Tales of the Broken Moon

the Bean's Song

Book 1

Written by Travis Hanson & Aimee Duncan
Illustrated by Travis Hanson

Bean Leaf Press

ISBN 0-9774127-0-9

Printed in the U.S.A.

First printing, November 2005

Cover illustrations by Travis Hanson

Special Thanks to Ray Bingham for the Glossary and Cathy Hanson for all the hours
of editing and nagging to get this done.

the Silver Dagger

The end has yet to be born. The beginning is forgotten. All that matters are the living tales, caught forever between yesterday and tomorrow.

An old path, overgrown and barely scuffed by the weary feet of travelers, meanders here and there through the forest of Darkleaf. It passes the door of a musty little inn, known as the Silver Dagger to some and to others, just a journey's stopover for a good brew, a bite to eat, and a bit of local gossip.

But that's only at first glance.

Ask anyone who knows the Dagger best. The praises far out-weigh the grumbles, but the wise newcomer takes all words of caution to heart... especially if he wants to be able to continue his traveling.

Strike up a conversation with the help if you like, but measure out your words as you do. There are many secrets kept silent behind a friendly word or a smile. Watch both your back and your purse. Nimble and quiet fingers have no sort of conscience around the careless.

Sample a drop or two of the eldenberry wine if you're feeling thirsty. Just remember...it's not always ripe.

But most importantly... pay the bill. Always pay the bill, my friend, for of all the fearsome beasts and crafty foes that lurk deep in Darkleaf's heart, waiting for the unwary traveler... none can compare with an ogre who has been cheated of his rightful coin.

***

"BEAAAAN!!!"

Gort scowled and shut his money purse with an irritable jerk of the strings before tucking it away again. His eyes scanned the crowd in the Inn this afternoon as he made a note of every fool and beggar along the way.

"BEAN!" the ogre shouted again. "Where be that blasted whelp? BEAN, COME HERE!"

Across the room, an untidy little scruff of a boy with straw-colored hair anxiously navigated through the aisles between the tables, carrying a heavy-laden tray in his arms. He stopped in front of Gort with a clatter of dirty dishes, pots, and mugs.

"Yessir?" asked Bean.

Gort frowned down at the boy. "Took you long enough," he grunted.

Bean adjusted his load to a better position as he replied hurriedly, "I'm sorry... got busy and then..." He stopped and thought a minute. "Never mind," he mumbled, dropping his gaze to the floor. "What do you need me to do, Gort?"

"Never mind?" echoed Gort suspiciously, "Out with it, boy."

Bean briefly glanced in the

8

direction he had come from. "Thought I overheard something about my father," he mumbled again. "Wanted to find out some more."

"Bah! Forget about him, boy. Told you, didn't I? Nobody wants to be bothered by your nonsense questions. Get to complainin' to Gort, they do. Bad for business, you know."

"I'm sorry, sir."

"You should be," said Gort, jabbing Bean in the shoulder with a huge grubby finger. "Care for you, I do. Think I wants you to end up like them? Eh?"

The ogre lowered his voice a bit and made a broad gesture that indicated the whole room. "Take a good look at 'em, Bean. All lost in their own worlds... broken worthless midden-heaps. Bah! Not a one of 'em's done an honest day's work like I have, I'll wager. They spend their hours drinkin' and dreamin' of fool's gold, searching for treasures that never existed, heirs to lies. That was your pap, too...You be listenin' to me, boy?"

"Yes, Gort." It wasn't a complete lie... Bean knew the words, having heard more variations on this lecture than he could remember. An awkwardly balanced mug on the tray he carried dribbled a thin thread of leaf brew down the front of his shirt, creating an almost welcome distraction. He winced slightly when Gort gave his ear a tweak and tried his best to look more interested as the ogre continued.

"Couldn't be trusted... him nor them. The Inn's the best place for you, boy... better off here, safer. Ol' Gort treats you good now, doesn't he, boy?"

Bean sighed and nodded.

"Treats you good, feeds you well. Most others like me'd knock you around, work you like a slave, yell all the time..."

Bean almost asked what Gort's idea of yelling was, before he remembered that the ogre's normal tone of voice tended to scatter the ravens nesting on the roof on a regular basis. For the sake of his smarting ear, the boy held his peace.

"I'm your pap now, boy. What's with that look, huh?"

Bean instantly made his face blank. "Drink's spilling on me, sir," he said. He earned yet another tweak for his poor ear and nearly dropped his tray.

"An' ol' Gort's an elf," the ogre growled. "Bah. More than a father actually... I own you. Sold you to me, your pap did to repay his debts. Worthless skunk his whole life an' he stuck me with you. So mine you are and mine you'll be... don't be forgettin' that." Gort sighed impatiently and rubbed his face. "Now, my little rat, stop this gnawing at Gort and Gort's good-payin' customers, scrounging for stories of the dead. I gets tired of it after a while. You understand, Bean? Eh? Don't know how to talk?"

"Yes... sir," said Bean, a little louder.

"Good. Bother me or the customers again and I'll take the broom to you. Gets back to work."

Bean turned away, readjusting the heavy tray in his arms.

"Bah! Come back here, Bean!" Gort snapped suddenly, stopping the boy dead in his tracks again. "Got me talking and made me forget what I called you over for."

The boy hurried back once more. Gort silently indicated a wretched excuse for humanity slumped at a table not too far away from where they stood. The fellow held his scraggly grey head in that peculiar wobbling way that told any casual observer he had long forgotten about everything outside of the next drink. His hands curled protectively around his mug as if he were afraid it might run off.

"Pay a visit later tonight to the ranger's room," said Gort in an undertone. "See what gifts you can find for Gort."

"But..."

"Ah-ah!" interrupted Gort. "Miserable sot stiffed me twice already on the ale. Owes me, he does. Payment from one thief to another. Now get."

He sent Bean on his way with a light cuff on the back of the boy's head that jostled the tray he carried. Bean caught it just in time and a piece of slimy gray gristle slid off a plate somewhere and landed on his nose. Bean's head shrunk down in his shoulders and a frown darkened his face. He shook the bit of gristle off of his nose and made his way past the counter. Behind it, Siv the barkeep quietly cleaned out a mug, set out another couple of bottles for a waiting customer, and watched the boy go by.

"...hate it when he does that, hmf... almost got me killed last time," Siv heard the Bean mutter, "Oh, I hope you drink a lot to-night, you old Ranger..."

The barkeep sucked at his teeth thoughtfully, pushed back a bothersome piece of white hair, and knelt down behind the counter to place the mug back with the rest.

"Well... none of my business," he thought as another customer tried to barter for a free drink.

***

Bean shouldered the heavy tray as he slipped past the greasy curtain draped over the doorway to the kitchen. He gave a little hop to one side to avoid getting trampled on as a rather irate young woman came in behind him, clanked down a tray on the counter, and grabbed a nearby ladle. Bean bit his lip at the appalled glare on her face and made his way to the sink as quickly as he could to unload everything. If anyone was fixing to catch a knock from that ladle she whipped around like some heaven-forged spear of wrath, it wasn't going to be the Bean.

"Groggle!" she growled.

A cleaver buried itself with a dull thump into the ribs of a partially butchered sloth carcass. The large gray ogre scratched behind his ear and finished pulling the ribs apart with his broad hands. "What now, Ravna?" he grunted, not looking up from his task.

"Groggle, you need to be more careful!" said the Mistress of the Inn, as she dangled a dead stew-soaked rat directly in front of his face. With a sigh of disgust, she dropped the rat on the floor with a splat.

"Groggle is always careful, Ravna," the ogre protested, waggling his cleaver and sending dark droplets of blood everywhere. "Respects the food, I do... that's the secret to good cooking."

Ravna stepped back quickly to avoid getting spattered.

"And what about the rat then?" she said tapping her foot impatiently. "What do I tell the merchant who found this in his bowl, hmm?"

"Just for flavoring," said Groggle, doing a poor job of hiding his amusement behind a slightly injured tone. "Only missed that one, usually they never know."

"Well now I know, Groggle. We want to keep our customers, not scare 'em away, so I'll thank you to keep your delicate ogrish ideas about fine cuisine out of the Inn's stew-bowls." The ladle poked the ogre hard in his chest.

"Humph," grumbled the old ogre with a sulky look, as he rubbed his chest and smeared his blood-stained apron even worse. "Picky humans. Too good for us ogres. Try it, you should... you might like it."

"I think not. Is that fresh batch of stew done?" Ravna dumped the bowl out on the floor and snatched up her tray again, tucking it under one arm before stalking over to a large pot bubbling over the fire. She sniffed it suspiciously, stirred it a bit with the ladle, and looked sharply over at the ogre.

"Ain't no rats in it," muttered Groggle. Ravna turned away with a frustrated sigh, failing to catch the mischievous grin that touched the corners of the old ogre's mouth. With a quick dip into the bubbling mess, she swept up a hefty and meaty scoop into the wooden bowl and tidied up her tray.

"And clean up this place, would you?" she added coldly over her shoulder, as she gathered up her skirt, daintily stepped over the puddle of stew in the floor, and sauntered out through the curtain again.

Groggle sighed to himself and tossed another discarded piece of meat into a nearby bucket. "Cranky. Cranky everyone is today. Ravna... Gort. Bah," grumbled the ogre as he continued working on his sloth. He glanced over at Bean, nearly up to his shoulders in suds, as he stood at the sink, washing up the dishes.

"Ah... good lad, starting on the dishes. Smart boy, you are. There's a big crowd in the Inn tonight, so much to do, yes indeed." Groggle nodded his approval.

"Mm-hmm," answered Bean absently as he worked. The ogre raised an eyebrow.

"Just 'mm-hmm'? Usually you make Groggle's head hurt with all your talking. Cranky today too?" Groggle asked in a deceptively casual tone of voice while he wiped his cleaver on his apron, laid it down, and picked up another knife to work on the flank.

"No... just thinking," answered Bean.

"Thinking? About what?"

"About my father." Bean's blue eyes carefully followed a soap bubble, as it drifted lazily up to the ceiling and popped.

"Ahhh," said Groggle wisely. He jabbed the knife into the wood of the counter and picked up his discard bucket. "Wicked ol' scoundrel he was, Bean, like Gort tells you. Good for nothing, lot of bad talk about him."

"What kind of talk?" asked the boy. He picked up a dish, examined it closely, and scratched at the egg drying on it.

"Bad talk, boy, like I said."

"Grog-gle," Bean protested. "That doesn't tell me anything. I want to know." He heard Groggle sigh as he scraped around in the bucket.

"Little lads can know too much sometimes," the ogre said.

"Twelve harvest-moons isn't little," said Bean, as he turned away from the sink and gave Groggle a deeply resentful look. The ogre shook his head wearily, made his way over to the stove, and scooped a greasy handful of something unidentifiable out of the bucket to toss into a smaller kettle seething nearby. He then took a meat hook off the wall and headed back to the chopping block.

"Wicked blood in your pap, Bean," he said slowly. "Talk was that he took a weaved gem from a dead king. And there's them that says he killed the king for it as well."

Groggle twisted the hook into the sloth carcass, hefted it up, and went to go hang it beside the other sides of meat. Bean turned back to the sink and started scrubbing out one of the pots, as he listened to the ogre continue, "So the king's ghost hunts the ol' fox, but Groggle's thinking your pap's a ghost by now as well. Bad thing, a weaver's gem be, mm-hmm. A bad thing, indeed."

Bean paused in his scrubbing. Very quietly he asked, "Do you really think my father's dead?"

Groggle eyed a rat carefully making its way down one of the chains hanging over the stove. Taking no notice of the ogre as he silently moved closer, the rat balanced itself with a bit of difficulty, and tried to snatch up a fragment of meat bobbing close to the edge of the scum-lined kettle. On the third attempt, Groggle's hand came up and carelessly flicked the rat off the chain. It plopped down into the stew with a piteous squeal that made Bean wince a bit. The ogre chuckled grimly to himself.

"Wouldn't surprise me. Be some folk in this world born for no better end than face down in a gutter with a dagger between their shoulder blades. And even a fate like that'd be too good for the likes of your pap."

Bean chewed on his bottom lip and rubbed his forehead with his sleeve before he gave a half-hearted sort of shrug and went back to his scrubbing. The silence settled heavily on the kitchen until Groggle sighed again and said, "Look... Bean, lad. Better you are here, with us... Groggle, Ravna, Siv, even ol' Gort. Better too... that you didn't know your pap so well. Fate willing, it'll stay that way. Harsh but true, boy."

Bean stacked the pot up with the others. He paused.

"But... you didn't really know my father either, Groggle," he finally said. He twisted the sponge in his hands as he frowned thoughtfully. "None of you did."

A spoon flew over the boy's head from the ogre's direction and landed in the sink, splashing Bean and startling him out of his thoughts. He wiped his face and looked over his shoulder to see Groggle grinning broadly at him. A small grin spread over the boy's face.

"Thinking so much be bad for the brains," the ogre chuckled. His face grew a little more serious and his tone became kinder, as he added, "Let the past stay dead, lad. Groggle will watch out for you. I promise."

"Are you sure I shouldn't watch out for Groggle?" Bean said, still grinning.

"You can try, lad. Won't do you much good." Groggle turned back and sniffed the stew.

"Needs something," he mumbled to himself and disappeared through a nearby doorway that led down to the root cellar. Bean heard the protesting groans of the wooden stairs and Groggle muttering to himself as the ogre made his way down

into the gloomy pantry.

"Shrooms, yes... shrooms be good. Dargle shrooms... strong enough to kill any smell... let's see, hmm... dargle, dargle... d-a-r... ah, here you be. Hiding in the dark, eh my gray-skinned beauties? Needn't be afraid of ol' Groggle... squint an' I could be just another shroom, wrinkles, bad smell and all... just bigger, heh-heh," Pottery clattered against itself and then the ogre snorted loudly in disappointment. "All gone, they are? ohh... fah..."

A few minutes later, Groggle stuck his head out of the doorway. "Bean, I gots a job for you."

"Yes sir?"

"Leave them dishes for now and go to the glen. We needs more shrooms, my lad," said the ogre, as he came back into the kitchen, holding an empty crock. "Dargles. Not the dark brown ones now... them older ones give the stew a bitter taste. I wants the young ones, not quite big as your palm, kinda grayish, yellow gills, a little wrinkled."

"Yes sir."

Groggle set the crock aside and took a small burlap sack off the wall as Bean hurriedly pulled off his apron. He threw it to the boy, who caught it easily, grabbed his jerkin from the shelf, and made his way towards the back door.

"Oh... hmm, wait Bean." The boy halted in the doorway. "Methinks we might be low on goldenberries as well, so get some of those. Make sure they're ripe this time though or they'll spoil the brew! Bad batch they made last time and ol' Gort doesn't need to be crankier than he is already, eh?"

"Mm-hm. Dargle shrooms… goldenberries… all right," Bean repeated and took off outside. Groggle lumbered quickly to the door and watched the boy hurry up the road winding away from the inn.

"Don't dawdle, boy!" he called. "And watch out for the wolvms. With the snows coming, they'll be hungrier than usual."

"Yes sir!" Bean called back. He turned around and walked backwards for a bit.

"Nay, none of this 'yes-sir'-ing. You tell Groggle that you'll be quick and careful."

"Groggle, I'm always careful, you know that!" Bean rolled his eyes, then promptly bumped into the fence, knocking a rail loose with a loud clatter. He spun around in surprise, and then looked back over his shoulder to the ogre. "I'll be back soon, I promise!" he yelled and ran off. Groggle watched him go with his hand on his hip. "Huh… so you say, boy. So you say," he grumbled. "If you don't take it in your head to run off again." He rubbed his chin, snorted, and went back inside.

Riddles and Shrooms

Groggle's warnings seemed harder to take seriously on such an afternoon as this. A trace of chill in the air promised a cold night, but the sun still shone warmly through the latticework of limbs and golden-red leaves overhead. Bean walked down the path, dawdling as much as he could, of course. He broke into a brief run and scuffed to a halt, long enough to send several pebbles skittering in all directions across the ground with a well-aimed kick. A couple ricocheted off of the remnants of an old rusted earthdweller vent leaning haphazardly against the stiles. The hollow clang of stone against metal rang through the woods.

"Don't be dawdlin' boy... wolvms'll eat ya... be quick, be careful..." Bean mimicked Groggle's grumbles. "Silly old ogre... you'd think I was going off to Heartleaf or something." He picked up another pebble and bounced it off the vent again as he went by. "Don't get to roam around the woods every day. I'm going to enjoy it."

He stopped a minute and turned. He touched his nose absently, catching a trace of something on the air... something smoldering. Bean sniffed, glancing around carefully but saw nothing to indicate a fire burning nearby. He looked over at the old vent again. No earthdwellers lived below ground anymore, although he had heard travelers in the Inn claim to see eerie tendrils of smoke still trailing up from the vents every so often. He worked up his courage, walked back over to the vent, climbed up onto one of the stiles, and cautiously peered down through the soot-stained grill, listening and sniffing.

Only dead cavernous silence met his ears. The vent smelled of nothing more than flaking rust and mold. Bean sneezed and the sudden noise bounced down the vent and echoed away into darkness. He rubbed his nose again and after a moment, jumped down from the stile. The icy tantalizing thrill of exploring the dark unknown quickly gave way to slight disappointment and a bothersome tickle in his nose that yet another sneeze banished. His thoughts turned busily, filled with the spectral voices of long-dead earthdwellers twining together in ancient songs and the scratch of skeletal hands in the darkness far below his feet. He rounded the corner and seemed to vanish from view.

A bird called twice. Stone grated gently against stone as part of the path lifted up slightly. Eyes below in the darkness studied the direction in which the boy disappeared and a fragile thread of pipe-smoke danced up into the air...

Further away, Bean slid down off the edge of the path, jumped over a ditch, and swept through a patch of broom-grass nearly as tall as he was, sending a couple of little birds flittering into the air. He stopped to watch a beetle crawling up a sapling, then plucked up the little creature and walked on until he met the path again.

He amused himself for a while, turning his hand over and over, letting the bewildered beetle lumber hopefully across his fingers before he stopped at a fallen tree close to the path.

He let the beetle climb onto the bark, then picked up a small twig and tried to coax the beetle to crawl into the twisting maze-like patterns etched into the dead wood by hard-working scribe-worms. The beetle dug in its tiny legs and refused to budge, apparently having grown very suspicious of Bean by this time so the boy gave up and left the insect to its own devices.

The beetle pushed itself into a crack in the wood and a little skyloc slinked out from the roots where it had retreated earlier. It raised its head, took a quick glimpse around and scuttled up the tree, nosing about hungrily. It scrabbled eagerly at the crack, widening it with nimble little claws and teeth until it could poke its head and most of its long neck inside. It emerged again and between its jaws, the beetle slowly churned its legs in vain. The skyloc bolted down its prey with quick little jerks of its head and snuffled around the crack to see if it had missed any other tasty treat.

A shadow rippled silently over the fallen tree...

The skyloc skittered back into the roots again with an alarmed whistle. A minute later, it cautiously poked its head out. A stray breeze rustled the treetops, spiriting away the lingering pungency of sweetleaf smoke and a cold dry smell of must...

Further ahead near a weathered old fence, a herd of highland sloth slowly meandered out of the trees and across the path. Bean raised his eyebrows in surprise and stopped to watch them. As the last one shuffled out of sight, the boy ran up to the fence, pulled himself up, and leaned over the rail. He saw the creatures waddle down the gentle slope and start grazing through a thick patch of undergrowth not too far away.

"Sloth," breathed the Bean. "And so close to the roads, too! Groggle'd like that... I'll have to tell him when I get back from the glen."

Bean stuck a finger in his mouth and held it up to test the direction of the wind before he carefully swung under the rail and edged down the slope. Imitating the soft contented grunts deep in his throat and keeping low to the ground as Siv had taught him on numerous sloth-hunting expeditions, Bean kept his eyes fixed on the nearest one, a youngster probably no older than two moons and what Groggle called a "cuffy." Its dam browsed gently through a patch of chokercherries not too far away while the little one pulled down branches and stripped off the tender leaves.

Neither paid much attention to Bean until the boy managed to get within inches of the young sloth, close enough to barely brush its coarse greenish-gray pelt with the tips of his fingers. It gave a sort of irritated grumble and moved away, while the dam raised her head and grunted loudly. All the sloth paused and silently lifted their heads. They stared at Bean with bright dark eyes for a minute and then quickly raised up on their hind legs and clambered up whatever tree happened to be handy.

Bean stood up and grinned, watching them making their way to the higher branches. He then crunched back up the slope and for a change of scenery, walked along the opposite side of the fence for a few minutes before finally ducking under it and getting back on the path.

"Old sloth on the road
Red-bird's trill
Stack the wood, lad
For long winter's chill,"

Bean chanted softly to himself. He didn't count himself terribly clever for being able to sneak up on a sloth; they weren't the brightest creatures to begin with anyways.

"Still," thought Bean, "the cuffy would've made a nice pet... so long as I could keep him out of Groggle's stew-pot."

The glen lay uphill a few steps from the path, sheltered by a thick cluster of trees, low goldenberry bushes, and a large rock that absolutely needed to be climbed upon by a small boy. Bean

24

scrambled to the top quicker than a skyloc, then sat down on its edge and kicked his feet idly against the lichen-encrusted stone as he gazed across the quiet glen.

"Hm-hm and here you be, my gray-skinned beauties!" he said, mimicking Groggle's slow drawl as closely as he was able to without the deep voice. He grinned and hopped down into a huge patch of dargle shrooms thriving in the cool damp shadows beneath the rock. He folded his legs, sat down on the ground, and began picking his way through the dargles.

Swift and silent as the wings of an owl, a dark figure moved through the nearby trees, closer and closer towards the glen...

Bean looked each shroom over carefully, smelling and studying it before dropping it in his sack. "No soft spots, no signs of the yellow-must... yes, you look a nice bunch for the most part," he said aloud. "And there's plenty of you, more than I thought there'd be. Groggle ought to be happy. Maybe I'll get a creme-pastry."

A broad hand rested itself lightly against the trunk of a nearby tree on the edge of the glen. Ears turned slightly, listening to the boy talking to himself, as dark thoughts drifted together within a mind as fragmented and deceptive as a shattered mirror: "Ahh, yes. Hear it sing now... hear it sing... and here's the one I am to bring."

The hand slid away, scoring four faint nail-marks across the whitish bark...

Bean rolled one shroom around in his fingers a minute, squinting at it.

"Not so wrinkled... looks like you're going brown too," he mused thoughtfully and then tossed it aside. "No... better not."

He pulled up a couple more, inspected them, and flicked a daddy longlegs spider off one before dropping them both into the sack.

"I don't care to get the broom instead of a pastry," he said to himself. "Just because the stew got spoiled from... one bad..."

Bean paused in mid-thought. The glen had gone unnaturally quiet.

"..shroom..." he finished.

He sniffed the air. There, that odd burning smell again, but it seemed so much stronger this time. Very strong. Almost as if it came from... right... behind... him.

A shadow fell across his back. Bean turned and stared up into shining yellow eyes. The boy didn't even have time to gasp.

Knuckles like iron slammed into the side of his head, knocking the boy sideways against the face of the rock. Bean slumped gently across the ground and lay very still, his breathing shallow and slow. A thin trickle of blood trailed down the side of his pale face.

The creature stood in silence, his dark cloak hanging on the breeze, as he studied the unconscious boy sprawled out before him. Then he took the pipe from between his teeth and tapped the bowl thoughtfully against the back of his wrist. He chuckled, a soft deep sound filling the watchful silence of the glen with unmistakable menace.

"Gone a-hunting for shrooms in the golden fall? Not a wise thing to do... ahh... not wise at all," murmured the red rock troll, as he snuffed his pipe, knelt down, and tapped Bean on the side of the nose with the stem. Tucking the pipe away, he dropped a large leather sack beside the boy.

"For now see how easily, young hunter of shrooms, that the hunter becomes hunted and himself is consumed?" he said, as he slid the bag over the boy's head and pushed him inside. "All trussed up and shushed in a snug leather sack..."

He hefted the bag up over his shoulder.

"...A useful gofer... tossed on my back," he finished with an unpleasant sneer. "Now home to Me-lonar..."

He walked calmly out of the glen into the trees, humming sporadically to himself. The air clung to him in faint shimmers and dappled sunlight moved silently across his shoulders, as he made his way through the undergrowth, deeper into Darkleaf, carrying his precious burden. Gradually his hums unfolded into a thread of soft mutters. As the hard lines of concentration faded from his forehead, his voice rose and fell under his breath, mirroring a subtle tempo spun from echoes of betrayal and ruthless ambition.

"Hm... hmm-hmm... yes... so dream while I scheme far into the night. Slumber deep below ground from day's cheerful light... hmm," he chanted gently to himself. "Tis a fine venture upon which we embark... a mission, yes, a quest through the brooding dark to far far below where dead memories still grow among stones ever cold, where bones lie under pale moss and mold. There it glows, waiting there... wreathed in voices of old. Ah... the song..."

He paused, and tilted his head, his eyes sliding shut as his sight turned inward. He listened to the whispering of the darkness within his mind, while all around him the everyday sounds of the living forest continued on, no more aware of his presence than he was of theirs.

"The song," he repeated, his eyes still shut as his expression drifted into serene enthrallment. "Alas... the song."

A flicker of pain suddenly overshadowed his face.

"Even now it draws me along," he whispered. "Steeped in the

stones within the halls of my keep… a melody haunting, so strong and so sweet. Like a dagger so bold… how it twists in my soul, the thorns guarding close that tenderest rose… with power, with strength… that devours as it grows. So must I yield…"

His eyes opened and grew hard as he stared down at the forest floor.

"Yet I shall avenge me first," he said, his tone gone strangely flat in sharp contrast to the lyrical ramblings of earlier. "The soul weeps. The blood wails and all shall be answered for… in vicious ways."

He spread out the fingers on one hand and swept them absently through the air, wiping away inner visions in one pitiless smear of purifying blue fire. He then shifted the sack to his other shoulder, glanced back up and continued on his way once more through the hall of trees winding away ahead of him.

The afternoon sun had faded into shadows of twilight when he stepped carefully off an embankment onto the remnants of another old road that had long ago ceased to exist for anyone except him. He felt his burden stir and his brows lowered. He set the sack on the ground, opening it to study his prize a moment. The unconscious boy lay quietly in the curved leather with his arm draped across his face. The creature reached down and snapped his finger sharply next to his ear. He nodded in silent satisfaction when he got no reaction, closed the sack and swung it up and over his shoulder again before he continued on.

Tall marker-stones, worn and green with age, leaned precariously over the road every few miles or so, their carvings worn and meaningless. The mute stones themselves were strangled by tree roots that twined endlessly down near the cloaked stranger's feet. Like deformed fingers, the roots clawed into the earth beneath the road, methodically breaking apart the paving. The road had become rough and untrustworthy over the centuries, but even in the failing light the one trudging down it now did so without a stumble or misstep. After all, how well he knew dark treacherous ways.

Over the passing of hours as the evening died, the shattered moon slowly rose into a sky crowned with stars. Far below, night began spreading velvet-gloved hands through the ancient trees.

Here on this part of the road, the forest turned ruthless in its efforts to overcome what remained of civilization's touch. Smaller paths trailed off into obscurity or ended abruptly at the foot of a tree. Bent and twisted armatures of rusted metal, their origins and functions forgotten, thrust vainly out of the upsurging undergrowth on either side of the road like the hands of drowning men. Pallid shafts of uncertain light danced across a cracked wall as roots slowly devoured it from inside out and one empty window wept thorny vines as it stared at the dark figure passing by, the outline of his shadow distorted by the bulky sack bumping and jarring against him.

Occasionally the rustle of some small creature, the soft sleepy buzz of an insect or some other nighttime noise could be heard, but his ears registered none of these sounds. He strode along through an eerie silence that existed mostly within his own mind. Finally his steps slowed and he stopped as his hand deliberately reached out in the darkness and touched a broken stone pillar close to the road on his left. His heavy burden slipped down to sag in an untidy heap by his feet. Like one struck blind, he kept his eyes fixed steadily ahead of him as he traced along the worn bumps and crevices, his hands remembering intricate carvings and the familiar runes of a dead language. He lifted his gaze and studied the closely-interlaced branches over his head, bleached white by the moonglow, casting tortured shadows across his face and the path.

"Rafters hung with blossoms sweet. On the pipers play. Dancers turn and dancers laugh and sorrow fades away," he spoke to the night. "Now the fire red is cold and dead. The pipers silent as stones. Flowers wither into black and the rafters are hung... with bones."

His fingers tensed on the pillar and his face twitched. "So very quiet. So still." He turned his ears forward, straining to hear something and then he smacked the stone with the side of his fist.

"The song fades," he hissed between his teeth. He stepped quickly away from the pillar and turned in all directions, tilting his head and listening intently. His demeanor grew agitated as he paced down the road for a few steps, then stopped again to gaze up at the sky.

"Mantled in moon's timid light," he spat. "Under a ceiling of bones, all twisted and white. How the years have turned and my rage has burned, yet for peace and quiet I will never yearn. Promises, promises they all made, but promises could not avert the blade. Their silence mocks me... where is the music? Who deadened the singing, the voices ringing under the carved archways ... where... is... the song?"

His hand tightened then relaxed gently. His maddened scowl faded into an impassive mask and he nodded as if coming to some sort of conclusion.

"No... no, bide a while yet. Patience. It will return... it always does," he reassured himself and in a more tranquil mood, he picked up his bundle once more and walked off on to a smaller path branching away from the main road. The air around him by now had grown damp and he splashed carefully through dark water pooling in the wayside. He smirked in anticipation, shifting the dead weight of his sack to the other shoulder. His footsteps quickened to match the pace of his rapid mutters.

"So dance and play while you still may. Sing your foolish lives away. For soon the music and laughter will fade and debts to the piper must be paid. The sun grows cold, the rivers slow, all choked with blood from the noble and bold... their finery decayed to worthless slime, their faces ashen and smeared with grime, crying for mercy through their tears, their wailing falling on deafened ears. Then riddles become truth, sending message clear that one survived the dark red years..."

He ducked beneath the spongy fungus-riddled trunk of a fallen tree, the leather sack on his shoulder dislodging fragments of rotten wood as it scraped against the tree. He stood beside another large marker-stone detailed with more strange runes and carvings.

"Now my time of retribution draws near," he said under his breath. Before him at the brink of a vast swamp, an old footbridge curved over a creek of motionless black water edged with algae and cattails. Among vents drifting smoke, a huge old tree stood beyond the bridge, bearded with silvery-grey moss.

The slats creaked under his feet as he crossed the bridge. In the thick trunk of the tree stood an oval door of hardwood, its frame ringed with cryptic glyphs and the door itself reinforced with iron bands and rivets. He pulled up the latch and the door swung silently open.

"Home again, my little gofer," he chuckled, swinging the sack in front of him and giving it a cheerful shake. "Home again. Dawn raises its axe and night shall be hewn. Then I alone shall call the tune. My day to play soon... so very soon."

The darkness eclipsed them both as he closed the door behind him with a soft click and his hums trailed away into the everyday sounds of the night.

an Evening Snack

"... eleven... twelve... thirteen..."

Siv picked up his mug, sipped reflectively at the ale, and counted out the day's profits behind the bar. More and more as the years went by, he found himself appreciating the peaceful hours of late evening in the Silver Dagger after the last traveler had retired to his quarters for the night, sometimes needing a little guidance from his well-meaning companions. After all, stairs could be tricky to maneuver for a fellow who had been on his feet for most of the day, this having nothing to do with the lack of seats at the bar-counter, of course.

He heard the door in the back of the kitchen swing open and slam shut again, followed by the voices of Ravna and the ogre.

"Groggle I understand. Honestly, I'm as concerned as you are, but you shouldn't be off wandering the woods at this time of the night..."

"Hrmph. Gots my cleaver, I do." The sharp firm thump-thump of the blade rapped against the chopping block, followed by the ogre's listless snort. "An ol' ogre can take care of himself in the woods 'specially against wolvms or any other beasts. But the Bean, he be only a little lad... oh, Ravna. Feel so bad, I do... that he's run off again. No... no, should go back out. Something's not right, no, not right at all. It all smells wrong..."

"That's just your stew, Groggle," Ravna's forced laugh rang out from behind the curtain. "Oh, don't look so sour at me... I was just trying to help you feel better. Look, it's not your fault... Now, let's just think calmly for a minute, Groggle. Bean's done this before and he always comes back on his own. Why... I'll bet he's just wandered down to the homesteads again... Probably ended up staying with Marathur and Mayve for the night. The earthdwellers will look out for him..."

"No, he wouldn't have done that... no, Ravna. He knew I needed his help tonight."

Siv heard Ravna sigh. Then she said, "All right Groggle. Maybe I can ask Siv to help us out. He knows every tree of Darkleaf down to the acorn, after all."

A doubtful grunt came from the ogre. "Don't know why you like that one so much. Barkeeps should talk more than Siv does... he's strange, too quiet... watching everything with those dark eyes. I don't like how he and Gort always be at each other's throats."

"Yes, but he does know things, Groggle."

"True... won't deny that. Hrmph. I still thinks you be soft on him."

"Oh, Groggle, really..."

A quiet amused smile touched the corners of Siv's mouth, as he continued counting out the bits.

"Even if you manage to convince the barkeep, ol' Gort will notice both him and the boy gone. And there'd be

36

more trouble," the ogre's voice added darkly and Ravna laughed.

"You are a silly old ogre. I know how to sidestep Gort. Now... please don't worry."

The rest of the conversation drifted on for a while longer, but Siv tuned it out to concentrate on his task once more. At this point, he had pretty much heard all that he needed to hear. Besides, two more bags of glass and steel bits sagged together on the counter waiting to be sorted and locked away in the strongbox he kept hidden behind the bottles of elderberry brandy. Siv's hand reached past his mug and closed around a worn black leather hilt lying on the counter. He shifted his sword a little closer to him. Even with money so temptingly close, stray travelers stumbling in after decent hours tended not to be too inquisitive of an armed barkeep.

"twenty-three... twenty... four... hm..."

He picked up a small jade bit and rolled it between his fingers thoughtfully. Then without turning his head or otherwise giving any sort of acknowledgment, he quietly remarked "How are you tonight, my dear?"

"Always the observant one. Was it the clamor of the curtain being pushed aside this time or did you just see me with the eyes in the back of your head?" Ravna smiled slightly, as she walked up behind him carrying a wedge of cheese, some fruit, a few slices of bread, and two small bottles of ale. She placed it in front of him before sliding in beside him and resting her chin in her hand as she leaned on the dark polished wood.

"Actually it was the sound of your eyelashes blinking that gave you away," deadpanned Siv, as he held the jade bit up to the light of the overhead lantern and examined it. "Hm," he said again.

"Hm?"

"Yes. Hm. Someone isn't as rich as they make themselves out to be or else they've been duped." Siv picked up another jade bit and tapped them together. "Glass." he confirmed with a nod.

"How can you tell?"

"Real gemstones make a different noise when they're tapped together." Siv rolled the bit around in his palm. "Bit lighter. No variation in the color. I'd guess the Pale Leaf merchant from this morning... he did seem strangely generous with his tips. Now you haven't answered my question yet, Ravna. How are you tonight?"

"I'm fine," said Ravna and pushed plate and bottle towards Siv. "Here. I know you were too busy to have a decent dinner this evening. I brought some leftovers from the kitchen, ale to warm the bones and a bit of chit-chat to warm the soul."

"All very much appreciated. Thank you." Siv laid the 'jade' bit aside and bent down slightly as he swept the rest of them into a small leather pouch. "Now... what is wrong, my dear?" he asked when he had straightened up again.

Ravna shook her head in amusement as Siv refilled his mug with the contents of the bottle and started on the cheese. "There's no glossing over anything with you, is there?" she said. "Well... I was just talking with Groggle in the kitchen. It's the Bean. He's gone missing again."

"Really." Siv swallowed and nodded to himself. "That's not so unusual, especially with that boy."

"Well... it's just upset Groggle a lot. More than usual this time. You know as well as I that old ogre's a lot fonder of Bean than he admits to."

"And he wouldn't be the only one, now... would he?" said Siv, giving Ravna a wise look as he passed her a slice of bread. She sighed and picked unenthusiastically at it.

"Yes... he's not the only one," she replied. "I just thought..."

"...You could maybe ask me to help you out?" Siv took a swig of his ale. "Well... I do know every tree of Darkleaf down to the acorn after all. Though 'tis most likely Bean's gone down to the homesteads. Wouldn't you think so, my dear?" He enjoyed the brief look of astonishment that crossed her face before the obvious answer came to her.

"Siv!" she exclaimed, partly indignant and partly amused. "I thought you had better manners than to eavesdrop on a conversation! Really..."

Siv arched his eyebrows. "Mistress Ravna, I assure you I am the epitome of genteel behavior," he said. "Was it I who was listening too closely or you that were talking too loudly? Hm?"

Ravna lifted her eyes to the rafters and waved her hand in a graceful gesture of exasperation. Then the smile on her face fell away again and she looked down at the piece of crumbled bread in her hand as unpleasant thoughts darkened her mind. Siv finished his meal, took out his stone pipe, lit it on an overhead lantern, and puffed away in the uneasy silence for a few minutes. He watched the sweetleaf smoke drift across the room and disappear, then cleared his throat a bit.

"So Groggle's worrying himself sick over the boy, is he?" he finally asked in a gentle voice.

Ravna nodded and laid the bread off to one side. "He's blaming himself. Apparently they had been talking in the kitchen about Bean's father before he sent him out. Groggle's convinced that might have been part of the reason for Bean running off this time."

"That makes sense."

"But Siv... there could be wolvms or who knows what out there in Darkleaf. That's Groggle's fear as well."

Siv chuckled and patted Ravna's hand. "Groggle would blame a wolvm if he couldn't find the apple butter. They'll be deeper in Darkleaf off to the south about this time of the season anyway, following the kithdeer herds."

"But... they aren't predictable creatures. You of all people ought to know that. What if..." Ravna grew quiet again, unable to finish. Siv shrugged and smiled.

"What of it? Do let us cast all hopes to the north wind and only expect the worst, Ravna. Give the little scamp a bit of credit. Hasn't he worked his way through some rough scrapes before? I mean... look how he handles Gort. Running away's not such a bad idea sometimes. On days when that ogre's raking me over the coals, I'm tempted to do it myself."

"Yes, I know, I know. But still... won't you do something?"

"What, pray tell, would you have me do, my dear?" Siv asked kindly as he gave his pipe a bit of a wave. "Weave him out of thin air?"

"No... but..." Ravna rubbed her forehead and looked down at her hands. "Since I've met you one of the things I have grown to admire about you is that you've always known what to do... where to find things... how to survive even when all odds are against you. You're one of those folk who... who can turn over a rock on the most barren of peaks and find roast mutton and a flask of leaf brew underneath. Please, Siv..."

"How very simple and dashing you make those skills sound, young lady," sighed Siv. "Yet 'tis one thing to find a missing bottle of eldenberry wine and another thing entirely to find a little boy. Especially if he doesn't want to be found."

Ravna's gaze hadn't moved from her hands. "Please..." she murmured again.

Siv rubbed his chin and looked sideways at her. "Deadlier than knife or spear, those sad eyes of yours are," he said and then his expression softened as he laid his hand on her shoulder. "Between a moping ogre-cook and a worried inn-mistress, I suppose there's no room for an unwilling barkeep. Very well then... I'll see about tracking down our little rambling vine yet again. So quiet your fears, mistress."

Ravna glanced up at Siv again. "It feels different this time. I... I can't really say why, but it just does," she said softly.

A reassuring smile crossed Siv's face. "Haven't I always taught you that a grain of faith is worth far more than a golden heap of doubt, Ravna? Think of what has always been the key to your survival."

Ravna's eyes grew tender with emotion. "Faith," she whispered.

"Indeed. So... hold onto that. Believe that the Bean's safe under a roof somewhere, snoring with a belly full of soup. Believe that you can hold your ground here, come Gort or high water. Trust in your own skills and abilities, young mistress... as I know that you trust in mine."

"Flatter yourself you do, barkeep. I'd as soon trust in mule-spit," rumbled a deep hard voice across the room that killed the conversation where it stood.

A massive shadow loomed out of the darkness at the top of the stairs and the steps creaked as the ogre made his way down and lumbered towards them. Siv's eyes immediately hooded over. He took a short drag on his pipe, laid it down, and turned his attention back to the night's earnings.

"Good evening, Gort," he said, his words cool and polite. "Wandering the Inn a bit later than usual this evening?" The ogre stood against the table and laid a hand as broad as a bear's paw on the polished wood, as he glared down at the barkeep sorting through the bits.

"I keeps what hours I please and none your business it be either." Gort's beady eyes shone unpleasantly. "Only waiting on my lad, Bean, to tell him a nice beddy-time story about a poverty-haunt-

ed ogre and a drunk old freeloader. But seems the whelp's gone scarce on me. Know anything about where he might be, barkeep?"

"No."

"And why not?"

"...three... four... Because I don't. Why don't you ask your brother? Bean spends more time with him than I do."

Gort's face darkened. "Mayhaps I did ask him, barkeep. Mayhaps he told me the boy was off doing something for him and ain't come back yet. Be you who's supposed to keep an eye on the little rat and tell me his comings and goings, instead of me having to find out for myself."

"Mayhaps I'm not paid to be the boy's wet-nurse," Siv replied evenly, as he dropped glass bit after glass bit into a little sack and counted under his breath. Ravna heard Gort grit his teeth, saw his neck go purplish with suppressed fury, and watched his hand squeeze into a white-knuckled fist.

"Here it comes," she thought and braced herself as she edged away.

"GARRRRRRRRRRRRRRGGGGGGGHHHHHHH-HHH!!!!!!"

With one explosive sweep of Gort's burly arm, everything on the counter went flying onto the floor. Glass and steel bits scattered everywhere along with the shattered fragments of bottle and plate. From the split mug, ale had spattered across the black leather of the scabbard and ran in brown rivulets along the length of the partially unsheathed blade. Through the trembling droplets of ale, a stylized rose of enameled jet and mother-of-pearl glimmered on the shoulder of the sword.

"GONE! Gone be the little rat and gone be my chances to get my hands on his pap's stone!" bellowed Gort, mere inches away from Siv's stony eyes. The ogre's meaty hand closed around the barkeep's shirt as Gort held Siv in a blistering glare.

"If you had been watching the boy..." he grated out and stopped. The metal-capped stem of Siv's stone pipe poked him meaningfully right underneath his chin.

"This works as well as any dagger, ogre, if you know where to jab it," said Siv in a deadly calm voice. "The world is full of if's, Gort. If I hadn't been off wasting my time as you like to call it, in the woods that morning all those years ago, then a certain bounty hunter and his fellow ruffians would have made events turn out badly for you on the road to Pale Leaf. We both know it... don't we, ogre? I suggest you let me go."

Gort's eyes narrowed to slits and he slowly released Siv's shirt. "Never asked you to help me. You should know how hard an ogre is to kill."

Siv smiled thinly and lowered his pipe as he got up from the bench and stood on his feet to face Gort. "It wasn't so long ago that one could get four steel bits for an ogre's scalp. Considering how cheap that is... it makes sense that someone perfected the means of dealing with such difficult creatures as yourself, Gort."

Gort snorted and returned Siv's smile with a cruel smirk of his own.

"Times be changing, Siv my lad," he chuckled, as he prodded Siv in the shoulder. "Ogre scalps ain't worth much to anyone anymore except mayhaps the ogre himself. Yet I hear the goblins still pay a pretty price for a flayed human hide."

"Do they?" Siv said softly. "Well, well." The barkeep's fingers closed around a stray steel bit as he rested his hands on the table. "Isn't it good that I earn my keep around here then..."

"Bah. I don't see you earning it now," Gort tapped the side of his head and nodded knowingly. "Thinks I his pap came back and snatched the boy from fear ol' Gort were gettin' too close."

"Somehow I doubt that. It's been seven years since the old codger dropped him off. Don't you think that if he were at all worried about that he would have tried to take back the Bean long before now?"

Ravna looked up at Siv as he spoke this and felt quite frankly amazed at the amount of self-control the barkeep exuded. Aside from restlessly rolling the bit between his thumb and forefinger, Siv stood perfectly still with an expression of such detached calmness on his face he could put a weathered old gambler holding a winning hand to shame. Yet the edge in his voice and his eyes, keen and alive as a biting north wind, made Ravna wary. She stood up to gently take his arm and felt the tenseness of his muscles beneath the sleeve.

"Prove me a fool then, Siv," sneered Gort. "Thinks you to find the boy, eh? Go on then... find him. It hardly be asking much from the way you boast... forestwalker." The ogre stabbed his finger in the center of his palm. "You keep Gort happy. You keep gold crossing my hand. Then no more squabble between you and I... Simple as that."

Without waiting for a reply, Gort abruptly turned his back on Siv and waved a disgusted hand in Ravna's direction.

"See that this is all cleaned up before first light, Mistress Ravna," he grunted and waddled off.

Ravna glared daggers at Gort's retreating figure. She moved away from Siv, knelt down on the floor and for a few minutes she

worked in furious silence, plucking up the fragments of the plate and dropping them in her apron. A shadow fell over her and a hand closed firmly around her wrist.

"Don't you dare..." came a steel-edged growl from Siv. Ravna glanced up and saw the barkeep glaring in the direction that Gort had disappeared.

"Stupid fat ogre," Siv muttered. Ravna sighed and carefully pulled her hand out of his grasp.

"It's nothing personal and you can't just leave this mess here, Siv," she said. "Bite your tongue and let it pass. Gort's been foul all day long." Her hand closed around the pommel of the sword as she briskly slid it back in the scabbard and pushed it towards Siv. As he picked it up and got back to his feet, she fished out a fairly clean dishcloth and tossed it up to him.

Siv sighed through his nose. He moodily wiped the ale off and in a swift graceful movement unsheathed the sword and laid the scabbard to one side as he took a minute to check its balance and clean the blade. Then he silently knelt down on the floor with Ravna and began gathering up the bits scattered everywhere across the well-trodden floor of the Silver Dagger. The fire hissed and muttered to itself on the hearth.

***

Like diamond dust on black silk, the autumn night sky glittered with stars. The moon herself, a sadly damaged pearl for all her beauty, hung over the horizon. Her broken light cast crisp shadows across the ground and precisely etched in silver every splinter on the Inn's sign and every leaf and twig of the nearby trees.

Behind the Silver Dagger, Ravna discarded the last pieces of the shattered bottles in the refuse pile close to the woods and shook out her apron. She pulled her cloak closer around her, walked back towards the Inn, meeting Siv shoving his arms through the sleeves of his coat on his way out the back door of the kitchen. One look at the expression on his face told Ravna all she needed to know. With a sigh, she gently stepped into his path and caught him by the elbow, stopping him in his tracks at the doorframe.

"I thought you had called it a night, Siv," she said. He gave an off-hand shrug.

"T'would be a shame to stay indoors and let such a pleasant evening pass by unappreciated." He replied. "Besides which... there's the Bean to find."

Ravna didn't answer for a moment, only shook her head and motioned Siv to turn more towards her. She pulled his coat tighter around him and fastened it up, kindly, but firmly waving his hands away. He finally dropped his arms and took it all complacently.

"Gort got to you again, didn't he?" she said in a quiet voice.

"He has a certain talent for abrasiveness many a grindstone would envy... if that is what you are asking, young lady," Siv answered as Ravna took a moment to tighten up the baldric of his scabbard. She stepped back and looked steadily up at the barkeep.

"Wait a moment and I'll see about finding some trail rations to send with you," she said, and Siv smiled faintly.

"Don't bother. I can find what I need and I don't plan on being gone long."

"Yes, but you must admit... bugs and leaves get rather dull after the first few days," said Ravna with a grin. "Don't go anywhere."

Siv nodded and as Ravna vanished inside, he clasped his hands behind his back in a dignified manner and tilted his head up to gaze at the sky while his breath frosted the air. In a bit, Ravna returned with bread and dried meat carefully folded in cheesecloth which she gave to

him.

"And your pipe and some extra sweetleaf," she said, placing it in his hands.

While he packed it all away in a small haversack on the side of his belt, Ravna leaned her back against the stones in the wall and looked up at the ends of the crossbeams lining the edge of the roof, poking out here and there from the straw thatch. Far behind her, on her left, the tower extended high against the stars. Every weathered inch of the Silver Dagger reassured Ravna of its stability. She enjoyed the quiet with the solidness of the wall at her back and the warmth of the absent sun soaked deep into its stones and felt quite grateful for both; the warmth especially, in the wake of the cool night breeze.

Siv studied her before lifting his eyes again to the stars. "Look there how the Seven Hunters chase her," he said, making a slight gesture towards the sky with his pipe.

"Chase her?" Ravna murmured.

"The moon." Siv's shadowed fingers danced across the heavens as he outlined another star constellation close by. "Her protector, the dragon Talithar, sleeps during these long winter months, so they pursue their wounded quarry while they can, always hoping to catch her... to finish what was started so long ago." He frowned. "If I remember my star-lore correctly... this will have been the closest they have come to her in several generations."

Ravna gave Siv a glance of frank admiration. "I think I know all there is to know about you and still you constantly surprise me." She smiled as she walked towards him and joined him in staring upwards. "Remember that old farmer's comment, those months back when you were impressing him with the finer points of planting by moon-signs? 'Do th' very stars an' moon talk to 'ee, barkeep, that you be a-knowin' all this?'"

"Certainly. All the time," Siv raised his eyebrows rakishly as he also glanced up at the sky and appeared to seriously contemplate the heavenly bodies for a second. "In fact, young lady, they're telling me something right this very moment."

"And that would be...?"

The barkeep passed his hand dramatically in front of him. "That... tis late and far past time for decent old ale-slingers such as myself to be asleep. And the moon and stars never lie." He grinned, but Ravna saw a flicker of weariness in his face and eyes.

"You don't think you ought to wait until morning?" said Ravna in concern.

"In a few more hours it will be morning anyway so it doesn't matter," said Siv. He rubbed her arm reassuringly. "Go get a bit of sleep, Mistress Ravna, you need it far worse than I do. Bean and I will be back before you know it." He looked up at the sky again and a look of disquietude crossed his face.

"A rare occurrence, indeed. The more superstitious might view it as foreboding." He stared into the dark shadows under the trees, listening and thinking, as hard lines creased his forehead.

"Siv," said Ravna quietly. He turned his head and Ravna smiled. She took his arm, motioning for him to lean down and gave him a tender kiss on the side of his face.

"Take care of yourself," she whispered.

He nodded at Ravna with a half-smile and a brief embrace took care of any further words between them. Siv then walked off down the same path Bean had taken that morning, rubbing the back of his neck thoughtfully. Above them over the ragged fringe of the silver-frosted trees, the moon peered like the milky eye of a dead man.

the Collector

"A broken moon... a silver spoon..."

The fragile shadow of moth trembled fitfully in the pale light of the gently turning lantern. Directly above it, with its tail and nimble little feet curled securely around the chain, the skyloc watched with steady unblinking eyes. One quick misjudged snap, however, did not bring a meal to the little hunter but only sent the moth fluttering out into the darkness beyond the lantern light. The skyloc slunk up the chain and vanished into the leaf-heavy branches of the ancient oak tree to follow its prey.

"A knife of brass... a golden glass..."

Attracted by the warm golden glow of light beyond it, the bewildered moth circled the grating near the top of a smaller door built into the north side of the oak's massive trunk. The skyloc edged its way silently up the door, but when it had come just within striking range, another sleek little head darted out from the grating, caught the moth and ducked back inside. The skyloc skittered after its thieving brother amid a flurry of outraged whistles.

"Onyx eye of a long-dead king... A serpent's tooth... a crystal ring...."

The slender little shadows pursued one another relentlessly down a short flight of wooden stairs lit by a few overhead lanterns that led into a larger staircase of flat stones and packed earth. Roots wove themselves into arching ceilings and writhed like fat worms along crumbling earthen walls flanking the winding stairs. Instead of lanterns here, clear stones of various shapes and sizes could be seen at intervals pressed into the walls in odd patterns, giving off a faint glow that illuminated the stairs, as they descended further into obscurity.

On the bottom landing stood another door, one of rusted and bolt-studded iron, and here hunter caught up with thief and a nasty little tussle resulted. The skyloc nipped and scratched viciously at the other skyloc, which had its mouth full of madly fluttering moth and couldn't defend itself properly. Finally, after a moment, the dying moth fell and the battered thief slunk back in defeat with a piteous trill. As the moth quivered in aimless circles across the floor, the skyloc triumphantly snatched up its hard-earned prize and wriggled through a crack close to the bottom of the door to find a quiet place to enjoy its meal.

"In a realm so fine with wealth divine... All nothing more than a quiet sublime..."

Beyond the iron door lay a foyer of white stone walls, unremarkable at a casual glance. Dusty bottles and jars cluttered together over the doorways, a stone box or two lurked in the corners, and strange-shaped pieces of badly corroded metal lay scattered across a worn filthy carpet that might have once been expensive and finely-woven in its day. Outside of the foyer, two more steps of stone led into a narrow hallway choked with impossible amounts of clutter, sprouting up in odd corners and spilling across the floor like the bizarre fruit of some noxiously flourishing weed.

"Now in dark old holes sleep dusty moles
While worms devour both book and scroll
Where mace smashed face and crushed trolls' bones
How the wails once clamored through the cones..."

The hall twined past walls hung with exotic and fantastically crafted weapons, ruined shields, and battered mismatched armor that sometimes completely blocked a doorway leading off into the dim unknown. Around a corner, one section of the hall had various helms hanging from chains attached to the ceiling and helms displayed on pillars, creating a disturbing impression of being scrutinized by hundreds of disembodied heads. Here too, as with the other items of warfare, these had been obviously put to use at some point in time, for all of the helms bore evidence of dents, holes from crossbow bolts, and splits from axe blades that left little doubt of the fate of their original owners.

"And here alone, in his underground throne
Watching... waiting for a song to begin
Once a melody so quiet and quaint
Little more than a nagging complaint..."

Underscored by a curious scratching noise just at the edge of hearing, like the soft sound of mouse's claws across dry leaves, the whispers and murmurs echoing down the hall grew more distinct in tone though no less mystifying in content.

"Yet how demure has now turned bold
And his oaths are sworn with powers old
Of promised wealth and blood-stained gold
Tainted in honor, weakened by grace
So rots a treasure of a forgotten race..."

In a dimly lit room adjacent to the hall, walls of dusty moldering books and tattered scrolls shared the narrow space with a few delicately mounted skeletons of various small creatures and several skulls. Quite a few of the latter of these natural oddities suggested an uneasy resemblance to more sentient species beyond mere bird and beast. Caught in the wan gleam of a lamp in the middle of the ceiling, the wired bones, yellowed and polished with age, seemed to glow inwardly with a subtle ivory light.

"Bibble and babble, chatter and whine..."

A shining droplet of rose-hued ink quivered on the sharpened point of a white quill as it was withdrawn from a small pot resting on the corner of a weathered desk. The hand that held the quill paused in midair as sweetleaf smoke drifted past.

"All fear this power, this energy mine..."

Fingers delicately curling around the stem of the quill tightened.

"...All mine..."

The point of the quill rested lightly on the smooth tea-colored surface of parchment, as he continued tracing the bold outlines of a curious looking diagram, dotted here and there with spidery notations written in a strange language. Yellow eyes narrowed in concentration.

"And how is it a call so sweet and so faint can mask such force and muster such strength?" mused a whisper over the busy and persistent scratch of quill against parchment.

" Hidden far beyond prying eyes
And only one can claim this prize

for the song binds it to the will, it does
ensnaring the soul, it devours with love. "

A grim smile flickered across the face of the red rock troll, as he dipped the quill back in the ink and finished the last lines of the diagram. Resting the quill on the edge of the ink-jar, he picked up another small jar, poured a tiny amount of fine sand into his palm and scattered it across the damp ink in a shower of grains that glittered in the lantern light. He gently blew the excess away and turned to another page half filled with more unknown writings.

"Still... love is not its only vice," he muttered as he picked up the quill again. "A vendetta unanswered it thirsts for, it fights..."

He grew still, his hand hovering between book and ink-jar. The point of the quill shining with dark red ink seemed to hold him mesmerized for a moment. Then his eyes flickered down to the parchment.

"Or so they say," he said quietly. "Still... one cannot tell these darkened days."

With a deep sigh, he rubbed the bridge of his nose and leaned back over his book to continue writing. He slid his pipe back between his teeth and pulled at it silently, his eyes darting back and forth across the lines of runes.

"Vengeance," he hissed as he wrote. "Vengeance for... vengeance... hmm?"

He slowly lifted his head and his yellow eyes shifted across the ceiling. His brows rose as he took the pipe from his mouth.

"Oh..."

Like honey over ice, a peculiar expression of longing and bittersweet hunger softened the edge of intense focus in his hardened face as the song lovingly consumed his mind once again.

"Heed how it calls, it shouts... nay, it screams! Time cannot waste on idle night-dreams," he said, clenching his fist in anticipation, as his eyes glittered feverishly. He closed the book, pushed his chair back,

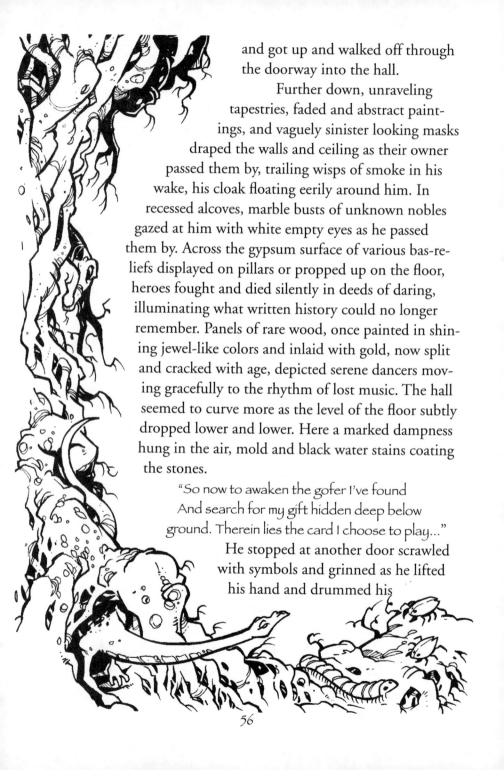

and got up and walked off through the doorway into the hall.

Further down, unraveling tapestries, faded and abstract paintings, and vaguely sinister looking masks draped the walls and ceiling as their owner passed them by, trailing wisps of smoke in his wake, his cloak floating eerily around him. In recessed alcoves, marble busts of unknown nobles gazed at him with white empty eyes as he passed them by. Across the gypsum surface of various bas-reliefs displayed on pillars or propped up on the floor, heroes fought and died silently in deeds of daring, illuminating what written history could no longer remember. Panels of rare wood, once painted in shining jewel-like colors and inlaid with gold, now split and cracked with age, depicted serene dancers moving gracefully to the rhythm of lost music. The hall seemed to curve more as the level of the floor subtly dropped lower and lower. Here a marked dampness hung in the air, mold and black water stains coating the stones.

"So now to awaken the gofer I've found
And search for my gift hidden deep below
ground. Therein lies the card I choose to play..."

He stopped at another door scrawled with symbols and grinned as he lifted his hand and drummed his claws lightly against the weathered wood.

"To amend the choices of an ill-starred day."

His grin became fixed and tight as he tensed his fingers.

"Heh-heh..."

Bitterness edged the clipped snicker. In one quick and carelessly vicious gesture, he swept his claws across the writing carved in the wood before dropping his hand onto the latch.

A fire snapped and popped on the stone hearth, but even its heat and light could not reach every corner of this cold dark and richly decorated den. The skyloc wriggled tail-first out of a crack in the ceiling from which writhed a fat white root. It scuttled down the root, which trailed and twisted along the length of the wall, interweaving with more roots emerging from various cracks and along the joints where wall met floor. As the skyloc leaped lightly onto the floor, it paused a minute to rub its snout against the stone and clean off white bits of wing and antennae still clinging to his face before it trotted lightly towards the direction of the hearth.

It wound itself between the legs of a wooden chair sitting before the fire, then started violently and took off at the sudden noise of a faint and painful sigh somewhere over its head. In the shadow of an ornately decorated vase filled to the brim with scrolls and standing by the fireplace, the skyloc's two bright eyes studied the small figure slouched and bound in the chair facing the fireplace.

"Eyes stared from behind a shimmering curtain of white hair, wise blue eyes as old as stone, as young as dawn. They closed and opened again. The eyes had turned black, the irises and the whites, the nauseous rainbow-tinted black of spilled oil that stared out from a mask of flawless white ivory. A woman's voice, low, soft, sweet, and filled with incredible pain, pleaded, pleaded with words he couldn't understand. Then the eyes wept tears of glowing liquid iron, smoldering in burning black channels down the smooth perfect ivory... he could smell the smoke and the mask

smiled as it wept..."

Bean opened his eyes and groaned.

Senses returned to him slowly one by one. He thought he heard the crackling of the Inn's fireplace as the smoke drifted past his nose and his mouth felt terribly dry. He wet his lips and wished the pounding ache in his head would go away. It made him want to vomit. Hazily, he wondered how he had gotten back to the Inn from... from... where had he gone again? His thoughts assembled themselves with some difficulty through what felt like the straw-filled ticking that Gort always grumbled about Bean having between his ears instead of a decent brain.

"Go... to the glen... dargle shrooms... an' don't forget the goldenberries..." the boy mumbled under his breath. He lifted his hand to rub his forehead and found he couldn't.

Tied to the chair? He tried his feet. Yes, they were tied too. He finally dared to lift his head; thankful it didn't roll off of his shoulders. His bewilderment deepened as he stared at an unfamiliar fireplace.

"Then the creature smiled... with its dark thoughts wild..." came a low murmur from somewhere beyond his sight.

"Huh?!?! Who's there?!?" the boy gasped, twisting his head around, his heart hammered faster in his chest. He squinted, trying to see beyond the wavering light of the dancing flames. A door stood open there.

"Hunting for a better way..." continued the voice serenely. "To toy with unsuspecting prey..."

"Who..." Bean's words caught in his throat. He swallowed hard and coughed.

A figure emerged from the slanting shadow of the door and took a moment to regard Bean with yellow eyes devoid of any kind of sympathy or concern.

"Tis only I.... no one less yet no one more," said the stranger. He bared his teeth in a frighteningly feral smile and walked towards the boy. Taking a drag at his pipe, he calmly exhaled sweetleaf smoke in thin threads between his clenched fangs. It wreathed around Bean, contorting itself in ominous and fantastic shapes. The stranger rested an elbow on the back of the chair and tapped the pipe casually against the arm as he bent down to eye Bean.

"So good evening, boy. How do you fare?" he asked the Bean. "Tucked away snug in my old wooden chair? The fire burns keen in the heart of my home... And so come I to warm me old bones."

He chuckled, slipped away from the chair, and stood at the mantle, rocking back and forth slightly on his heels. He studied Bean, who tightened his hands in their bonds and felt extremely uncomfortable underneath such a penetrating gaze.

"Who... who are you?" the boy finally managed in a hoarse whisper. "Why am I here? And where is here?"

The smile dropped from the stranger's face as quickly as if it had never been there. He gave his hand a bit of an irritated wave.

"Questions, questions he does ask," he muttered as he appeared to examine the pipe in his other hand. "Who am I and what is your task? Well... Some things I'll tell you... some I will not."

His eyes darted back towards Bean and he leaned forward a bit.

"So take heed... I never answer twice... And there's secrets about me that aren't so 'nice'," he said, spitting out the last word as if it were an obscenity. He flung out his hand imperiously to indicate the whole room, with its cluttered corners, odd-matched furniture, and rusted equipment as he turned himself to face the fire.

"A Collector am I, of artifacts rare... Of treasures discarded without thought or care," he said, giving the Bean a sharp look over his shoulder. He picked up a curious item from off the mantle, a smoky crystal in a black wooden stand, and as he studied it, a rose-colored glow appeared deep in the heart of the gem.

"You see, boy... precious gifts wait deep below ground... gifts of

prestige, gifts meant to be found."

He slid the pipe back in his mouth, inhaled, and breathed out smoke thoughtfully. "It is all about promises, young one... promises and power..." His voice dropped as he stared at the crystal in his hand.

"Power," murmured the Collector, "that calls with a song... pleading and pulling me gently along, telling me all I desire to hear, drawing me closer, drawing me near..."

His eyes slitted and he seemed to have forgotten both Bean and his surroundings. In the deepening silence, sparks popped out of the hissing flames and a fragment of glowing wood rolled across the stones of the hearth.

"What does that... have to do with me?" Bean finally whispered, his eyes watching the dying ember as it slowly faded to black. The Collector replaced the crystal on the mantle.

"Everything, boy... everything..."

The Collector turned around and his shadow stretched over Bean in his chair as he walked closer. Bean raised his head and saw the creature standing before him, edged in red firelight. The Collector lifted up his hand, keeping his face shrouded deep in darkness. In that darkness, two empty eyes shone like white-hot coals. Bean drew in his breath quickly as he felt a shift in the air around him, a sudden blossoming of ice through the stifling heat.

"A gofer you are, a gofer you'll be, burrowing through seas of darkness for me, to fetch back a gift, a song of a ghost, and return it to its proper host," said the Collector. In his open hand, a bluish glow crept across his palm and outstretched fingers, growing brighter. Bean heard the creature humming under his breath, a tuneless steady drone that grated against the boy's ears. Even as fear and confusion tightened his chest and dulled his thoughts, Bean found himself involuntarily tapping into a wellspring of courage from some unknown part of his soul.

"What if I choose not to?" The question finally forced itself out between his cracked lips.

The Collector lifted his head a bit and grinned silently. In his hand, the bluish white light had taken on a life of its own. It danced and twined restlessly across the palm, pouring out between his fingers like vaporous water, sending out little stray sparks as it steadily increased.

He chuckled. "A choice you think you have?"

He made a mock of seriously pondering the boy's question, tapping the side of his face with his finger and letting his gaze roam across the ceiling before he looked back at Bean, his bared teeth white in the shadow of his face.

"Maybe... maybe... ah, yes here they be. Here's the choices I'll give to thee," he said. "Tis all very simple, simple and straight. Mind now, the answers cannot wait. And a yes or a no will determine your fate. So think hard, boy..."

In the intense white depths of the lengthening light in his hand, shadows emerged and grew more distinct. A hissing bubbling noise filled the air as he gently let the light flow through his fingers into his other hand. It instantly solidified into a sharp and ancient-looking dagger and he gripped its hilt tightly.

"No one can find you, you're now all alone," he said softly, his cloak swirling around his legs as he circled Bean in his chair. "But choose ye wisely and I'll send ye safe home."

The weapon danced in front of Bean's face and the shadow of the dagger fluttered across the boy's forehead. Bean could see the cruel edge shining in the firelight, shivered and squeezed his eyes shut as his chin sunk quickly down to his chest.

"Pay attention, gofer," growled the voice of the Collector and flicked him lightly on the shoulder. Bean's head immediately shot up again and he watched the dagger.

"Two are your options, two they be. Option one states.... you come with me. Together with me, you'll stay alive... Together, you'll see... you will yet thrive," said the creature and leaned forward. "Or two...

stay behind. For me, that's fine..."

He shrugged, and the blade slipped quietly underneath the ropes crossing the boy's chest as the Collector held him in an emotionless stare.

"And upon your bones the rats shall dine..."

The edge of the blade pressed gently against his collarbone.

"As they say... the choice is thine..."

Bean could hardly breathe. The yellow eyes of the Collector overwhelmed him, submerging his resistance in their merciless amber depths. Finally the boy lowered his gaze to the floor.

"I don't want to die," he whispered. "I'll go with you."

The Collector smiled mirthlessly. He turned the dagger and with a quick savage jerk, severed the ropes.

"Excellent, lad. What a grand choice you've made," he said, his tone laced with irony. He then sliced through the bonds on the boy's wrists and stepped back, as Bean shrugged off his ropes and bent down to untie his legs. Bean grimaced, as the feeling crept painfully back into his deadened limbs. He had to support himself on the chair as he stood up, stamping his feet and rubbing his wrists to banish the prickling needles of discomfort.

"Let us be off for the hour is grave. Speed is of the essence here. So no dawdling, gofer, no doubt or fear. Now, come..." the Collector ordered sternly, the dagger dissolving in his hand in a flicker of blue-white flames. He walked briskly towards the door, humming to himself as the tattered edges of his cloak hovered in the air. The boy hurried after him leaving an empty chair and a dying fire casting shadows over the stones of the hearth.

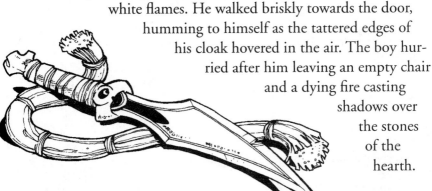

It seemed to Bean that he had been walking for ages beneath arched and vaulted ceilings that seemed to grow increasingly higher and wider the further down they went. For the first hour or so, his mind had been preoccupied with sorting through every possible means of evading this mad creature and somehow finding his way out of this nightmarish lair. But as he continued to be prodded relentlessly along in front of the Collector, he grew more and more confused with the endless twists and turns through the labyrinth of corridors and soon came to the realization that the hoped-for moments to break and run weren't going to come. Besides, he didn't have the first clue in which direction safety lay. Such a grim thought proved unbearably depressing and to distract himself from dwelling on it, he took to studying the assortments of odd relics crowded along the floors and walls. He began making a game of trying to guess what they were and almost found himself enjoying it, if not for the smell of the pipe smoke in his nose and the occasional curt order to "turn here, boy" or "no... not that door, the next one."

After a while even the orders and muttered threats fell into silence. Once in a while he felt an impatient nudge on his shoulder when he walked too slowly or stopped completely to study some interesting-looking instrument. When an intricate brass telescope draped in cobwebs in a dark corner caught his fascination for a moment, an irritated snort and a sharp cuff on the shoulder sent him stumbling forward again. Bean rubbed his shoulder ruefully and stole a glance at the Collector walking briskly beside him. Riddles and mutters hadn't told Bean very much, and the endless dripping of water and the rustle of creatures scurrying out of their path made a poor substitute for conversation.

"How... much further do we have to go?" Bean finally asked in a low voice. The Collector's fingers spun thoughtfully through the air as he stared ahead of them.

"Hm-hm... Crafty the tune, all woven in runes," he replied. "Double-edged the gift I see. Though lost to all, yes lost it be... Lost to the world but not to me... heh."

A smug smile came to the Collector's face. Bean stopped and watched him walk on, talking to himself. He realized the creature had not heard him.

"How much further do we have to go?" Bean repeated a little louder. The Collector stopped in his tracks and turned, his yellow eyes narrowing as he gave Bean a poisonous look. The boy suddenly felt nervous. Perhaps this unpredictable creature might have heard too bold a tone in his words?

"Until we get there," the Collector finally answered softly. He made a curt gesture. "Nasty things below here dwell. So listen, gofer, heed me well. Our hunt lies deep where dead things creep. Not all souls rest in peaceful sleep, so by my side, 'tis best you stay... Do this and you might live another day."

Bean felt his flesh crawl and hurried forward towards the Collector. The shadows seemed to have grown deeper and more sinister in their musty old corners. The Collector turned without a sound and the two of them continued walking with Bean doing his best to stay at east a step ahead of the Collector.

"And still it sings, the melodies ring, strumming and thrumming on the heartstrings."

Bean heard the Collector sigh to himself as they walked. The boy looked up at the creature again and decided to take a chance at conversation one more time.

"So... what is it you're seeking for?" he asked the Collector. The red rock troll gave his hand a bit of a wave.

"Seek... eh. We seek a stick, a little lad's toy, which once united and destroyed. Now it lies hidden far far away... feared and loved in the height of its day," he answered and held out his arm dramatically, as his eyes gazed far off into dreams of pride and glory.

"Calls me it does... I hear its sweet song. To me alone, it shall belong..."

Bean gazed at the serene expression on his face and almost, almost for a moment, it seemed his ears played tricks on him. It almost seemed that just on the edge of his hearing, the creaks, drips, and rustles came together in a faint and strange music, and suddenly... Bean knew. He knew as certainly as if someone had whispered it in his ear.

"A sword," he murmured to himself, stopping in his tracks. The Collector glanced sharply at him.

"It's... it's a sword isn't it?" Bean said triumphantly. His blue eyes shone with excitement at having figured it out. "A magic sword. It must be. How else could it call you?"

"How else, indeed," said the Collector quietly. He faced Bean now and his fingers flexed restlessly.

"A magic sword..." repeated Bean in wonderment and then quickly sucked in his breath as that same sharp cold sensation flooded his nerves once again. The Collector's hand glowed white once more.

"Magic... yes-ssss, magic it be, my dear foolish little gofer," he hissed mockingly under his breath. His eyes held Bean in cold amber contempt and Bean wilted under that stare. It told him that he knew nothing whatsoever of the deep and ancient powers slumbering far beyond the grasp of his innocent and untutored mind, powers that this creature standing in front of him could awaken and manipulate with the merest whisper or thought.

"Magic that weaves in and out of the soul. Scarring it, wounding it, taking its toll. And a powerful weapon this 'magic' blade be..."

A pillar of white fire leaped into life upon the Collector's palm and Bean saw its luminous blue heart waver and twist into the blurred and wavering image of a sword. Bean stared, captivated at the sight of the shadow-sword burning silently in the midst of the white fire.

"Aye... unique in her class, but alas... torn from the hand that wielded her so. Left in the cruel and bloodstained snow. Now sleeps and dreams under cold, bare stone..."

With the Collector's whispers wreathing through his mind, Bean moved forward, not even aware of his hand slowly rising towards the spectral weapon or the eagerness and awe in his eyes. The Collector saw it however. He knew the hunger and his eyes darkened in sudden distrust.

"Waiting for me... and me alone," he said in a deadly soft voice. His free hand trembled and then with frightening speed, it shot out like the talons of a hawk, catching Bean around the throat.

"So burn... this image... in thy mind... For the blade you seek... isss mine... ALLLL MIIINE!!!!!."

Bean's eyes whitened and his mouth worked frantically as the Collector lifted him with no apparent effort far above his head and shook him like a kitten. The deceptively gentle voice now gritted out between the creature's clenched fangs, a dagger's rasp against cold black stone.

"Long have I searched and wept for this blade," came the low growl. "And it's not for some... boy to take away. Steal my song and I'll

flay you alive. And hang your skin in the caves to dry..."

The wide yellow eyes shone wild with hatred and mad suspicion. Bean could barely breathe. He felt the claws digging in his throat and sparkling white specks floated in his vision.

"Do you understand me, gofer?"

"Yes... sir," Bean finally managed to wheeze.

"Well put, boy." With a snap of his claws, the fiery sword vanished and the Collector flung him carelessly against the wall and turned away with a swirl of his dark cloak. Bean coughed weakly and squeezed his eyes shut, grimacing as he rubbed his neck and the back of his head.

"Oww..." he murmured.

"Get up, lazy gofer. We still have far to go," grunted the Collector irritably. Bean hustled to his feet as quickly as he could. If he had known the right direction he would have run, but it seemed he had

to content himself with trotting hurriedly as close beside the red rock troll as he dared. He rubbed his face anxiously, walking and wondering if he would ever see the light of day shining through the shadows of branches, hear the scratch and whisper of leaves playing across the ground, or taste the cool autumn breeze again.

"Perhaps that's the reason why he's insane... from living underground for who knows how long," came the disturbing thought. Right after that thought came another one, even more ominous. "The longer I stay with him... will the madness infect me too?"

He had no answer; or rather he didn't want to know the answer. They had stopped again at an apparent dead-end and Bean watched the Collector push an old wooden globe with crackled and peeling paint inside a rusted ironwork frame away from the wall. The boy had to dodge a couple of rolled-up old rugs as they toppled over and hit the stone floor, raising clouds of dust. Bean sneezed and rubbed his streaming nose miserably. The Collector glared back at him.

"Quick now," he snapped. "Our time creeps away. Haste we must make for the sword will not wait."

He stripped a map drawn on moth-eaten parchment off of the wall, carefully rolled it up and put it off to one side and Bean realized they stood at a door. Only two carved runes marked the keystone directly above the arch. Bean had no idea what they said, but he suddenly felt weak with anxiety at what might lay beyond them. The Collector eyed him, a grim smile twitching the corners of his mouth, as he pulled open the latch. The door groaned, flakes of rust falling from the hinges.

"Gather your strength, gofer. You will need it," he said with a chuckle. He swept Bean through the door into the cool damp blackness waiting beyond. It seemed to the boy that the madness crept in behind them, eating up all memory of sunlight or sky.

Shrewd Bargins

Early morning in Darkleaf normally brought with it a sense of tranquility and peace as the first birds awoke and began trilling out their welcomes to the sun rising over the ridge of the trees. However, a song rather far removed from the liquidy warble of the oriole or the wistful murmur of the mourning dove could be heard echoing this morning along the little path to the Silver Dagger:

"...Then came Ogre King
So crafty and old
His eye a-glitter with wicked gold
And for him 'twas a sad fell day

When the goblin-children came to play.
So derry-o, tarry-o a while with me
'Tis lost to the world this poor cad be.

And the Elven Child
So noble and bold
His hopes destroyed by the ogres of old
Took him a blade and a price to pay

And avenged his blood in a terrible way.

So derry-o, tarry-o, lo-diddle-lee
'Tis looost... ahem-hem...
'Tis lost to the world this poor cad be...

So the Traitor schemed
While... hm... as... da-dee-dah-da something-strove.
And... and... something-something as the weavers wove...
oh... confound it... never can remember that third verse..."

Crimson Per frowned, his brown face looking much like a very annoyed potato with a beard. He tightened up on the left rein a bit as the wagon rounded a corner. A starling balanced on a slender twig above their heads seemed rather unimpressed and flitted off somewhere to add its voice to what it considered a much better morning choral.

"Might be a blessing in disguise there, pa," joked the tall young man sitting beside him and immediately got playfully swatted with a hat for his observation. Crimson Per jammed his hat back on his head and turned his eyes to the road once more.

"A son with no respect for the wisdom of the past is the shame of his old father's hoary brow, Fencer," grumbled the old man. He looked sideways at his son with smiling brown eyes. "And as I recall, 'twasn't that long past when you yourself sang right along with me, eh?"

"Oh, I have nothing but the deepest respect for those old songs," Fencer quickly answered. "But as for singing them... well... times have changed. You know that."

"Aye... times change," nodded Crimson. He scratched under his beard thoughtfully. "Years go by. Sons grow up... lose themselves in chasing a sunrise over greener pastures... become a bit forgetful of how they were raised, eh?"

Fencer smiled and shook his head. "Some sons, perhaps," he answered and gazed out at the trees passing by. "White Bird Cove... well, it has its good points. Always something going on... busy, full of life and color and bustle and excitement... but it's maybe too much sometimes. I remember where I belong. And it's good to be back. I find that Darkleaf refreshes the spirit."

"That it does, boy, that it does," Crimson agreed. "It's why I stay here."

"Funny, I thought it was Heartleaf's love of your sour-apple cider that did that."

"Well, that too my boy... that too." Crimson chuckled. "Ah, but I've missed our rides together. Out of all your brothers and sisters, only you ever had the patience to ride with me on my weekly rounds."

"Tannis seems to enjoy it."

"Oh he does, but he's a youngster yet. He'll probably follow in your footsteps when he's old enough. Still, he enjoys Darkleaf and the company of his family... though I wonder here lately if that little spinner's daughter has become as good an excuse to travel to Heartleaf as spending time with his father."

A hopfly landed on the back of Fencer's hand and he flicked it off as he sighed. "I still enjoy my family," he said, a bit defensively.

"You have to understand... it's too big a world to spend the rest of your life tending farms, chasing kids and haggling over brews and herbs."

Crimson pondered these words a moment. "You might be wise to the world in some ways, Fencer my boy," he said with a grave face. "But you still have much to learn about life. For example, it's about time you think about settling down..."

Fencer rubbed his jaw, which still had a shadow of stubble across it. He looked up at the branches passing over their heads and then closed his eyes serenely as he rested his chin in the palm of his hand. "Because this is the age most young lads start considering their futures..." he added silently to himself.

"...Because this is the age most young lads start considering their futures..." Crimson went on.

"...And learn to better appreciate the things that really matter, like an honest day's work and family..." thought Fencer.

"...And learn to better appreciate the things that really matter, like an honest day's work and family..." said Crimson with a firm nod.

"...And now he's going to ask if I've found a girl yet," Fencer concluded in the privacy of his mind.

"So anyways, what's kept your heart in White Bird's Cove, my boy? Some pretty little Velumni lass caught your eye, eh?" Crimson asked.

Fencer smiled slightly. Some things never changed.

"No lass, pa. So how much further to the Dagger?" he asked quickly to dodge the subject.

"Not much further. Just over that ridge. Twill be good saying hello to everyone again, won't it after five winters gone?"

"Has it changed much?" Fencer shifted himself on the wagon seat with a soft grunt of pain and began kneading his leg.

"The ogres are a bit crankier, but Siv still keeps them in line. Bean's not such a little fellow anymore. I'm thinking he's going to end up about as skinny as you, though far from as tall." The older Per's eyes twinkled a bit. "And Ravna's only gotten prettier with the passing years, you know," he added mischievously.

"That's nice," said Fencer absently.

"I'm sure she'll love hearing all about your grand city, my boy," Crimson continued hopefully. "All your daring escapades and adventures. Why you ought to tell her about young Lord Darrow and that night you..."

"Don't, pa," Fencer looked over at his father and his voice had gone cold and quiet. "I'm trying to forget that, all right?" He returned his attention to the trees passing by.

"All right," answered Crimson, snapping the reins and clicking his tongue at the mult-ox lumbering ahead of the wagon. "Gee-up there, Mab, the wine'll be past vintage at this rate." He whistled an old tune under his breath and stole a glance at his son as Fencer adjusted himself again. Crimson sighed through his nose, pulled his hat lower over his face, and turned his attention back to the road. Suddenly his expression brightened as the tower room of the Dagger came into sight. He nudged Fencer and cupped his hand by his mouth.

"HOY! DAGGER!!!" he bellowed cheerfully as the rest of the Inn appeared. Ravna emerged from the doorway, wiped her hands on her apron, and waved at them.

"Hello Master Per and a good morning to you!" she called back with a smile. The wagon pulled up to a stop by the sign and Crimson climbed down to tether Mab to the post.

"'Tis a wonderful morning indeed, young mistress," he replied with a nod.

Ravna's eyes briefly settled on

Fencer as he made his way slowly down from the wagon seat. "Who's this lanky fellow, a new hireling, Per?" The old man laughed and Fencer raised an eyebrow and sighed.

"The hireling be my boy, Fencer, home for a while to help with the harvest," he said and Ravna's face brightened with sudden realization.

"So it is! I almost didn't recognize him," she remarked and smiled at him. Fencer cleared his throat and pretended to be very interested in the reins suddenly.

Crimson Per turned back to Ravna, swept off his hat and took pains to smooth down his thinning gray hair. "So I just happened to be passing by the direction of the Dagger this morning, Mistress Ravna. I was wondering if there be any generous souls here willing to feed an old man's family or should I just push on to Heartleaf?" He looked hopefully towards the Inn.

Ravna's smile turned prim. "For an old man... oh I think we'll be buying today," she said teasingly and Crimson rubbed his hands. "Excellent, excellent. So might I ask where Siv is this fine morning? He usually makes the purchases. Sleeping off a long night behind the bar, eh? Small wonder you're in short supply of drinks," joked Crimson and Ravna laughed as well.

"No, Master Per, Siv went off on an errand last night. So... how much for six cases of leaf brew?" Ravna said briskly.

"Not one to waste time in small talk, I see. Three bits per bottle. Ivory," answered Crimson quickly, as a shrewd gleam came into his eye. "So you say Siv's gone? More's the pity..."

"Yes, it is a pity. And what do you mean three ivory bits per bottle?" Ravna automatically fell into bartering mode, as she put her hand on her hip and eyed Crimson. The old man sighed and looked mournfully up at the Mistress.

"Times have been tough, Ravna, lass," he began, rubbing the back of his neck. "You know as well as I how the hollow-stem blight has wreaked havoc on the honeyshrub fields this year, especially mine. A decent leaf brew is as hard to come by as hen's teeth. High demands and low supply, you see."

"Well, I am honestly sorry for your troubles, Per, but three ivory bits?" Ravna remained unmoved. Crimson sighed and waved his hand.

"All right, all right. Two bits and a glass bit, then. But I'm being more than generous."

"Two bits or you can take your generosity right down to Heartleaf and hope it doesn't sour on the way," said Ravna and waved towards the direction of the road.

Crimson scratched his nose thoughtfully. "Hmmm. Shine-fire, but you're getting sharp there, girl. Did that ferret, Siv, put you up to this?"

"Siv's taught me well, but I know enough about the worth of a good brew and an honest price," Ravna replied. "Two bits. That's your offer, Master Per. What do you say?"

Crimson sighed. "All right then, Mistress Ravna. Two bits." As Ravna smiled her prim little smile again, Crimson added firmly.

"Two bits, yet you'll have to buy an extra case of eldenberry wine to compensate me for my losses. Ten bits. Ivory."

"Five bits," Ravna shot back automatically.

"Nine and a glass bit."

"Four bits."

"Eight bits, then."

"Eight bits???"

"Eight bits and if you barter anymore with me, Mistress, you'll be getting the wine from the vat I fished that drunken skyloc out of the other night, I promise you that."

Ravna chuckled at that and held up her hands, shaking her head. "Fair enough. Toss in a couple of bags of dried yellow rumleaf for four glass bits and we'll call it a deal." She stepped back inside to get his payment, as Fencer climbed out of his seat and began unloading the cases from the back of the wagon.

After coming back with Crimson's payment in several small pouches, Ravna climbed up into the wagon, sat down, and pulled out the small wooden chest of herbs beneath the seat. Opening it up, she rummaged through the various linen bags of yellow rumleaf, sniffing them for signs of mustiness, and carefully picked out the ones that still seemed potent. She glanced at Fencer walking past with a crate of bottles and remarked, "So by the uniform I take it you serve in the military somewhere, Fencer?"

"Yup," said Fencer, carefully setting the crate down on the ground.

"Ah, don't be so modest, boy!" said Crimson, proudly raising his chin a bit as he motioned to Fencer. "Ravna, he's head yeoman of the personal guard for Lord Darrow, a Velumni noble in White Bird Cove and the Lady Darrow is first cousin to the king himself. Not bad for a young brewer's son from Darkleaf, eh?"

"Head yeoman?"

"Rather like a chucker for a bar, only I shave more often," remarked Fencer, without cracking a smile as he disappeared to the

81

back of the wagon again. "I've been with the family for five winters now."

"So what are you doing back in Darkleaf, then?" Ravna asked, sliding the chest under the seat again. She hopped down to the ground, while an awkward silence followed her question.

"Personal leave," came the terse reply. Another pause stretched out for too long, broken only by the clatter and clink of bottles against each other. Ravna leaned against the side of the wagon, twined her fingers together thoughtfully for a few minutes, and then tried again.

"So what's it like in the city, Fencer?" she asked brightly. "All the festivities… the parties… and the nobility?"

"Rather dull. Unless you actually enjoy those sorts of things." Fencer passed by her, carrying the last crate. He sat it down on top of the other crates and without another word, climbed back up into the wagon seat. He pulled out a dagger and a whetstone and began sharpening the blade, humming softly to himself.

"I'll take your word for it, then," Ravna murmured to herself with a raised eyebrow. Crimson sighed and made a show of straightening up the crates.

"Don't mind the boy, Mistress," he said in an undertone as his face softened. "He's had a rough go of it. Between all the tension going on in the south and… well… some things he had to deal with recently… you understand." He gave the crates a smart rap and said, "Well, there's your herbs, and seven cases of the finest my vineyards and fields have to offer you. 'Tis a shame, Siv wasn't around to enjoy your bartering skills. Where'd you say he was off to again?"

Ravna sighed. "Bean ran away again. Siv went into the woods to search for him."

Crimson clicked his tongue sympathetically, while he and Ravna walked back to the wagon and Crimson unhitched Mab. "Ah poor boy! Darkleaf's no place for a little fellow like him."

"I'm not worried. You know Siv. He'll find him safe," said

Ravna with a weak smile as Crimson took her hands and patted them in farewell. "Still... do us a favor and watch the roads, would you, Master Per?"

"That we shall, Mistress, that we shall. Have yourself a good morning now," said Crimson Per warmly, as he climbed back into the wagon. "Let's be on our way, Fencer. I'll be wanting to reach Heartleaf before midday." He took the reins and snapped them sharply. "Gee-up, Mab, my girl!"

As the wagon rumbled slowly back down the path, Crimson Per shook his head and made a tch-ing noise. Fencer ran the dagger up and down the whetstone.

"I'd run off too if I was forced to work for an ogre," he grunted. "Filthy creatures, all of them..."

Crimson frowned. "Fencer, mind your words."

Fencer looked over at him curiously. "They ran your grand-parents out of their underground cities, killed elves and the lost trolls, and you say 'mind your words?' Don't you dwell on that at all, pa? We'd been better off if they'd been wiped out all those years ago."

Crimson shrugged. "What happened in the past is past, son. Not even weavers can change it. I can't say I'm fond of ogres either, but Gort and his brother are just like any other folk in Darkleaf... just trying to survive and I respect them for that."

"Well, that might be the way you see it, but I still think them no better than the wolvms or the stone trolls or any other beast for that matter." An impatient tone crept into Fencer's voice. "You've seen the destruction, heard the tales... why, it's amazing that White Hall is still standing. King David ought to take the offensive for once, just attack and rid the mountains of all those filthy creatures. Yet they all sit around and harp about unity and mutual understanding and it sounds pretty enough written down on paper, but... Pa, they're too focused on peace when they should be thinking of prevention. Why the nobles say that the boy king..."

Crimson turned his head and stared Fencer down. The expression on his face and the sharp gleam in his eyes made the words die on Fencer's tongue.

"Is that the talk of the south then, my son?" he asked in a soft voice. "Do they really think the north so weak and savage, that White Hall is some worthless fragile trinket of glass and stone upheld in the tender hands of a boy king?"

"Don't put those words in my mouth, Father..." Fencer said wearily.

"Don't lie to me and say that thought didn't cross your mind." For that Fencer had no answer. He dropped his gaze and glanced back at the road as his father continued, "Son, there is so much more to the world of the north than endless violence and beasts. Would you wish a war upon the people of Darkleaf, upon your own family? That kind of talk, thrown out over fine wines from gold-powdered lips and such, is the kind of talk that starts wars. That 'boy king' as you call him is trying to find a way to stop wars from being the quick and easy answer to everyone's problems. Three nations have been destroyed by such 'solutions' in the past. He believes that there are better ways to broker peace than by violence. But mind you, even as the king holds up the crystal in his right hand, he keeps his other hand on the handle of the sword. If he needs to, he will fight for his freedom and the freedom of the folk of Darkleaf... including the ogres that survived the purge. He has the final say, my boy. He chooses what is best for all."

"But..."

"No buts my son. Only five winters since you left and in that time the people of Darkleaf and the king of White Hall have become no more than opinions and idle gossip over someone's dinner table. Hard to believe..."

Fencer sat back in the seat and said nothing. His father pulled his hat a little lower and snapped the reins again, urging Mab onwards. They both bore the uneasy silence until Fencer couldn't stand it anymore and tried changing the subject.

"You think they'll find the boy, pa?" he asked quietly.

For a moment, he wasn't sure if his father would answer him. Then Crimson sniffed thoughtfully and leaned back against the seat. "Hard to say, Fencer," he replied. "Hard to say. Lot of dark and nasty things out there in the woods. Fate willing, they'll find him soon. You never know what you'll run into in Darkleaf."

The wagon creaked onwards towards Heartleaf, as tensions slowly relaxed and father and son fell into lighter conversation on matters of no consequence. Somewhere far from the Silver Dagger and deeper in Darkleaf, a scuttling noise echoed out of one of the old overgrown earthdweller vents as a skyloc climbed out, landed nimbly on the ground and darted off further into the woods. Ten more minutes of its life crept by uneventfully, consisting mostly of scratching over tree roots and darting from shrub to shrub. On some instinct, the skyloc paused, raised its head, and stared curiously into the undergrowth with shining black eyes.

Bowstrings creaked, then released. Two soft hisses ripped through the silence of the forest. One black-fletched arrow ricocheted off of a rock far in the undergrowth and splintered. The other found its mark.

"Eep!"

The skyloc twitched helplessly, pinned to the ground, as dark blood trickled down into the soil. Then the little creature gave one final shiver and fell still, its shining black eyes staring sightlessly at the small hooded figures emerging from the bushes. Above Darkleaf, birds scattered into a sky smeared with pale clouds. Their faint cries could just be heard above the rumble of distant thunder in the darkening west. The clouds glimmered with swift and silent lightning and the air smelled of rain.

Into the Blackness

As delicate as spun glass, a hauntingly lovely chime flowered through the pressing damp darkness. The darkness yielded to a trembling golden glow that grew more distinct, even as the music increased and became sweeter. The light became stronger and the chime died once more into silence while Bean gazed down at the beginning of massive carved stone steps, thick with dust, and illuminated by elegant oval crystals set in slender staffs of delicately carved stone. He realized then that his world had opened up into possibilities both frightening and beautiful beyond imagination.

The Collector silently took his hand away from the crystal nearest to the door. Bean caught a brief glimpse of something shining on the end of a gold chain in the folds of his palm, a small curious instrument about as long as his forefinger. It looked like a miniature, blunted version of the fork Groggle used to poke cooking meat with. It disappeared within the folds of his cloak before Bean could get a closer look at it.

"Move, gofer," said the Collector. His voice echoed out beyond the glow, suggesting a vastness of incredible proportions lurking there waiting for them both. Bean bit his lip and reluctantly started down the twining stairs.

Every few steps, they passed another pair of crystals like the first one, crystals that slowly lit by themselves as that same sweet chime filled the air and faded. The Collector walked silently beside him, his cloak drifting behind him in an eerie wraith-like way. At the bottom of the steps, the last and largest set of crystals came to life, their pale golden glow intensifying to a blue-white light and a sudden gentle chorus of chimes fluttered up above their heads like a thousand shadowy butterflies. Slowly, luminance in a dazzling rainbow of colors emerged at the call of the chimes, blending together and sculpting the formless dark. Bean's eyes widened as a huge and endless underground city came into creation before his eyes, a wondrous place shining with splendid and vibrant life just on the edge of bursting into music and timeless voices...

The chimes drifted down into silence again and the illusion faded. Bean saw instead the stark reality of ruined skeletal buildings, empty windows, immense statues, and monuments all shattered, mute, and covered in the grime and dust of centuries. Here and there were patches of darkness where the carefully placed crystals, the source of the illumination, had either cracked or fallen out of their settings into obscurity. Pipes, many of them broken, rusted, or dribbling water snaked out haphazardly from walls and disappeared upwards in the arched stone ceiling. Here, too, the creeping moist organic life steadily reclaimed the caverns for their own, gnawing away at the bones of the decomposed city.

The Collector swept past him as Bean stared all around him, his mouth hanging open. He felt a hand catch him by the arm and impatiently pull him forward. Bean stumbled hurriedly along beside the Collector as they walked along a raised road winding past broken stairs and ruined houses. Still black waters shimmered just beyond where they walked and in some places, water almost completely covered the road. Bean stopped dead in his tracks and skipped hastily backwards when, ahead of him, something slithered quickly through a dip in the road filled with water and slipped quietly on its way, barely making a ripple on the surface of the cavern pools. The Collector stepped over the dip and continued on without even a glance down. Bean stared down where the thing had vanished, his face twisted slightly with distaste and he jumped quickly over the dip to catch up with the red rock troll.

The boy listened to the constant hollow drip of water and the faint scuttling of small creatures in the shadowed parts of the caverns that the strange unsteady half-light of the crystals could not penetrate. Sometimes further off in the caverns chimes would ring out softly as the crystals came on, set off presumably by some small resident of the underground. He startled once, as a chorus of booming calls echoed from somewhere further away, before he realized that it was the voices of the great sloth calling to each other. He remembered then that Siv had told him how the sloth retreated to the warmer underground when the weather began turning cold. Yet the calls, amplified and deepened here beneath the ground, along with the pale kaleidoscopic glow of faulty crystals fading in and out, only made Bean's surroundings all the more eerie. The lights especially, flickering through the abandoned buildings, set his all-too eager imagination conjuring up restless spirits clutching spectral lamps as they drifted through dusty rooms and down cracked steps, gazing down at him through the empty window frames. Trotting hurriedly along to keep pace with the silent red rock troll, Bean almost felt like a wraith himself; a small ghost keeping company with a creature spun out of nightmares and old wives' tales, the both of them wandering through a dimly-lit dream.

Still, when the boy didn't let his imagination turn his spine to ice, he kept finding himself caught up in the vast wonder of this place. He stepped over an intricately designed, but sadly rusted and shattered street lantern bent across the path, as his head turned this way and that. Far out in the pools, the half-submerged stone head of a statue turned its sightless eyes upwards like a drowning giant. Close by, the blinking glow of shattered crystals lit up a carved panel of scenes in the side of another building. Bean squinted at it, trying to make sense of the ruined artwork. He caught a glimpse of figures dressed in robes, carrying something underneath stone arches, but most of it was badly defaced and shattered.

The Collector abruptly turned off to the left and disappeared through a dark doorway partly blocked by the remains of a shattered and twisted door. Bean followed after him and climbed over the wreckage as best as he could, getting a nasty scratch on his leg from a splintered piece of wood in the process. He nearly lost his footing when the floor suddenly gave way to a set of stone steps. He swung his hands out against the wall to quickly catch himself and flinched when it came in contact with what felt like cold spongy moss. The red rock troll came back up beside him and helped steady him with a hand on his shoulder as Bean quickly wiped his hand on his vest with a whispered, "Ick..." Moments later, he felt very relieved when the Collector again struck a nearby crystal with the odd instrument he had used earlier and chimes rang out over his head as arches of light came to life in the ceiling and along the walls of the stairway corridor. Bean didn't relish the thought of feeling his way step by step through the thick darkness.

　　The silence began to bother the boy again. As he kept a couple of steps ahead of the Collector, his hand brushed curiously against the smooth clear crystals embedded in the stone as he walked down the curving stairs. His eyes caught shimmering threads of living gold that spun busily in the brilliant heart of each crystal. "Wow," he murmured with frank amazement as he followed the stairs around another curve. "I never knew such places existed down h..."

Bean stopped dead in his tracks and retreated so quickly he tripped and fell against the cold hard stairs. "Oh... oh my," he whispered, clench- ing the sleeves of his shirt tightly in his fists as he held on to himself and shivered. A skeleton in full armor sprawled in their path, blanketed in a thick shroud of cobwebs and dust. The steps beneath it were dark and filthy with decay. Several arrows protruded here and there through the armor and its outstretched hand clutched another broken arrow. The shadow of the Collector fell over the boy and the tattered edges of his cloak drifted around the boy's shoulder. Bean looked up and saw the still face of the Collector studying the skeleton. Something flickered briefly in his gleaming yellow eyes and his lips moved slightly.

"Ah... the reek of death... The paling bones," he finally said. "The fallen soldiers, all cold as stones."

He knelt down, pulled Bean up to his feet and stepped around the skeleton. Bean pressed himself up against the wall as he followed the Collector, trying his best to avoid touching the thing and trying in vain to avoid looking at the ruined face with its sagging jaw and vacant eye-sockets.

Yet death pressed closer against them as more armored skeletons appeared slumped over the stairs, each one spiny with arrows. The stairway opened up into a vaulted corridor hung with rotted tapestries and curtains, and Bean almost felt he couldn't breathe, so thick was the air with the smell of dry-rot and mold. Above a larger doorway, further ahead of them, the light of crystals mounted around a shattered stained-glass window softly fell on a scene of carnage that made the boy's stomach twist and turn. Hundreds of skeletal soldiers, larger than any human he had ever seen, their bones and weapons scattered across the stone floor, lay distorted and bent where they fell, dying in almost certain agony. With his nose in his sleeve, Bean followed so close behind the Collector he almost stepped on his heels. It seemed no matter which way he turned his head, the cruel reminders of this ancient slaughter kept intruding upon him. His imagination worked all too well, whispering stories to him about the last moments of this soldier slumped in an alcove with his bony hands twined uselessly around the shaft of a spear thrusting out of his chest or those two arrow-riddled skeletons, their backs to a moth-eaten tapestry that still bore the faint shadows of spattered gore.

"Did... did you know any of them?" asked Bean in a muffled voice.

The Collector stopped. He looked back over the corridor, his eyes darting over the walls and tilted his head slightly.

"The blood tasted sweet in their mouths, did it not?" he muttered between clenched teeth. "Yet I warned them. I heard the screams as they advanced... the screams and the laughter... and the singing, ah... the deep voices ringing. All silent now, all dead. By elven arrows they were felled and red ran the waters of the sacred wells. Yes, boy I knew them. Once they had names, carved in polished stones... forever now they are nameless bones. So they shall stay 'till the end of days... but revenge will yet be mine, my sons, for a battle lost..."

The Collector paused a moment as his eyes glanced back towards the foot of the steps from where they had come. For a few minutes he listened intently.

"...is only a war to be won," he concluded at length. Suspicion darkened his face and his yellow eyes hooded over as he methodically sorted through instincts and sensations running down forgotten corridors of his mind. He stood a while longer in the shadows, deep in his own thoughts, as Bean puzzled the meaning of his rambling words and wondered at his stillness. Abruptly, the Collector's expression cleared.

"A pity about the tapestries," he murmured, turning on his heel as he walked out beneath the shattered window. Bean looked over his shoulder with a final shiver as he followed the Collector. A few minutes later, the rows of crystals in the stairwell faded into darkness as something pattered quietly down the steps. A slight draft in the air stirred along the edges of the curtains.

Emerging from another doorway, they walked across a vast courtyard where huge white stalagmites studded with hundreds of darkened crystal lamps, rose near its center. Near the top of another set of stairs, magnificently wide and inlaid with gold and blue tiles, the Collector lit up another set of large crystals. As the chimes sang out and the brilliant bluish-white radiance filled the darkness, one by

one the crystal lamps lit up until Bean felt as though he stood at the feet of mighty trees, watching flowers of light burst into brilliant enchanting life before his eyes. Surrounding the courtyard, walls of tall slender mirrors reflected and enhanced the effect of the lamps until this section of the city looked as though it was almost illuminated by daylight.

Yet Bean could see the still figures in rotted armor stretched out in the shadows, the framework of crumbling buildings standing out starkly in the light of the lanterns, the shattered windows and cobwebs, and the signs of death, destruction, and ruin that continued to mar the unearthly beauty of the underground city. Many of the mirrors were chipped, cracked, or lay in shards across the courtyard. Bean glanced over at the Collector as they walked down the stairs past several bodies.

"What destroyed this place?" he asked.

"Elves, boy, with weaves untamed. Ever on and on they came, flaunting their might in the underground, weaving through trollish cavern and towns... and devoured us beneath the ground," replied the Collector with a bitter edge to his voice.

"I... always thought elves were... peaceful and didn't bother anyone," Bean said. The Collector glanced sharply over at the boy.

"Thought you wrong, gofer," he hissed. "With troops they came, with sword and lance, and slaughtered those who fought the advance. Naught, but the dead and restless souls dwell here now in the world below, here in the darkness, in the endless cold. Only I choose to remain remembering those who fought in vain..."

The Collector narrowed his eyes, sighed, and turned from the boy as he continued on. They now traveled another wide raised road beside a broad shimmering lake that looked as though it had flooded out much of the city. Foundations had crumbled, leaving buildings to slide helplessly down into the midst of the broad waters. Here huge pale vines rampaged through the caverns, twisting around statues and monuments, draping over alcoves, choking fountains, bursting from walls, and twining around the ever-present stalactites.

As they walked, Bean watched the red rock troll and thought

of the years, perhaps even the centuries, that had rolled by for this creature, as he had lived out his life with a lichyard of a city rotting away just below him; knowledge that had devoured his mind even as underground scavengers had gnawed at the decaying bones of his people. Bean wondered about those people the troll had known, who had had names, who had laughed, sung, talked, and created such rare and beautiful wonders. All at once, as he pondered on these things, understanding briefly dawned on the boy and in a moment the sadness and the horror of it all overwhelmed him and made him feel weak all over. As he looked up at the Collector, he grasped briefly why madness could be a mercy and sanity a burden... and it scared him as nothing ever had before.

"I'm... sorry," he whispered to the creature's back and his voice trembled in the darkness.

"Eh?" The Collector stopped in his tracks and turned to give Bean a very hard stare.

"I'm sorry," Bean repeated. He swallowed hard and cleared his throat. "For what happened..." he added in a slightly stronger voice.

The Collector raised an eyebrow. "Save your pity," he said levelly. "You cannot understand what you feel sorry for."

"But... I can," said Bean. "In a way... I guess..." His voice fell silent under those passive yellow eyes. A sudden stillness hung uncomfortably in the air as the boy and the red rock troll regarded each other.

"No, child," the Collector finally said in a soft dead voice. "You cannot." He turned back and looked deep into the darkness.

"Compassion is merely a fault of nature... a weakness to overcome. Only remember it cannot save you... or the world either," came the bitter murmur over his shoulder and the Collector continued walking.

Bean folded his arms tightly, rubbed them briskly, and then hurried to catch up with the red rock troll. The significance of the exchanged moment gradually faded for the boy and he took to staring at the walls as they walked by. He could see a skeletal arm or the

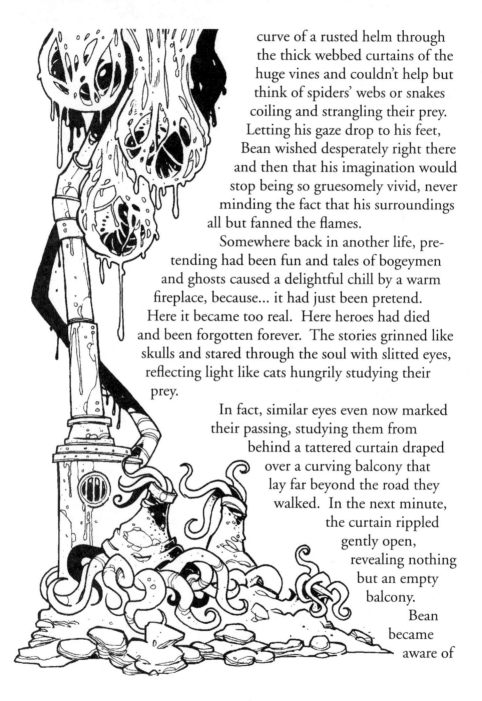

curve of a rusted helm through the thick webbed curtains of the huge vines and couldn't help but think of spiders' webs or snakes coiling and strangling their prey. Letting his gaze drop to his feet, Bean wished desperately right there and then that his imagination would stop being so gruesomely vivid, never minding the fact that his surroundings all but fanned the flames.

Somewhere back in another life, pretending had been fun and tales of bogeymen and ghosts caused a delightful chill by a warm fireplace, because... it had just been pretend. Here it became too real. Here heroes had died and been forgotten forever. The stories grinned like skulls and stared through the soul with slitted eyes, reflecting light like cats hungrily studying their prey.

In fact, similar eyes even now marked their passing, studying them from behind a tattered curtain draped over a curving balcony that lay far beyond the road they walked. In the next minute, the curtain rippled gently open, revealing nothing but an empty balcony.

Bean became aware of

a steady faint roar just on the edge of hearing as they passed under a carved archway into the beginning of another series of corridors that became narrower, darker, and more cave-like the further they traveled. The air became damper here and water dripped constantly from the ceiling. Faintly luminescent funguses of all sizes and shapes sprouted everywhere and when the boy accidentally tripped on a perfectly round white one the size of his fist; it burst open with a soft "whoof!" sending up a shower of glittering spores into the air that drifted around like dazed fireflies before attaching themselves to the walls and ceiling. He absently brushed away some that stuck to his pants and stifled a yelp of pain. They were as spiny as thistles and hurt twice as bad. He stuck his stinging fingers in his mouth and watched a pair of mullgrubs crawl by on multiple legs. They were bigger than he had ever seen before. Something sticky dripped suddenly on the back of his hand and he absently pulled his fingers out of his mouth to wipe it off, wrinkling his nose at its pungent smell. Looking up to see where it had come from, his eyes widened to see huge semi-transparent sacs hanging from the cavern ceiling and glowing a faint sickly green. Shadows moved silently within the pulsating sacs, shadows of creatures he didn't want to see any closer than they already were, and he moved carefully away from underneath them to the farthest edge of the road.

They turned a corner as the road followed alongside a broad creek. Bean watched water sheeting down from several screened drainage pipes into the creek and often saw some sort of water-loving beast rippling sleekly through the dark creek. The roaring sound grew even louder

as they crossed over a small wooden footbridge that led them through another corridor. After continuing a while through absolute darkness, Bean felt very relieved when the narrow passage broadened suddenly in front of them. He saw a pale-blue light streaming through a doorway up ahead, curtained in shining threads of flowing water. He picked up his pace, swept eagerly through the water as the joyous pounding roar completely swallowed up all his senses.

Bean stood with wide awe-filled eyes, rubbing the side of his face as he tried to take it all in. He was standing in a cavern, by far the biggest one they had come through, with vaulted ceilings miles and miles above his head, and to his left a massive waterfall plunging down the stone sides of the cavern walls. He stood at the beginning of a long narrow stone bridge that looked absolutely flimsy in comparison to the vastness of this cavern and the majesty of the waterfall. Bean slowly dropped on his bottom and stared all around him. The Collector strode past him and gestured impatiently, so he carefully got back to his feet again and followed, feeling too much like a beetle on a fragile twig.

Bean could dimly see the end of the bridge ahead of them and it seemed impossibly far. A thick cold mist drifted through the air and in no time, the boy's hair hung heavy and wet on his forehead. Water trickled down the sides of his face as the cold mist saturated his clothes. Bean constantly shook his head, ruffled his hair, and wiped his face to no avail. He watched beads of moisture travel down the sides of the Collector's cloak as if it were made of a sleek oilcloth. The Collector continued walking, seemingly unaffected by either the damp or the cold. Bean sighed unhappily, as he pulled his hands into his damp sleeves and tucked them tightly underneath his arms. He stole a glance down at the white frothing teeth of the falls far below the bridge and caught a glimpse of scattered ruins of buildings and shadowy piles of rubble and pipes. He immediately wished he hadn't looked down. He could feel the powerful relentless pounding of the churning waters vibrating through the solid stonework of the bridge and the constant roar in his ears, and it didn't reassure him one little bit.

At last the bridge ended and as they ducked into another doorway, the noise of the waterfall grew soft behind them. They passed through a small room filled with curious instruments, levers, gears, switches, and a latticework of rusted pipes, criss-crossing over the walls. Bean couldn't help but be reminded of a more complicated version of Groggle's massive stove in the kitchen. Everything lay draped in mold and spider webs. Bean reached out to run his hand over a lever in a panel of levers. Black dust clung to his fingers as he took his hand away and he saw the shine of carefully inlaid, but badly tarnished silver, twining in a wonderfully intricate design over cracked and peeling leather and worm-eaten wood.

"Careful boy, among things so old," warned the Collector behind him.

"How old is all this stuff?" Bean asked, as he thoughtfully rubbed his fingers together.

The Collector made a dismissive gesture as they moved on through the narrow room. "Oh... ancient it is... older than bones from before our time in ages unknown," he said. "Yet worry not of times long gone. 'Tis my quest you should focus on. That and nothing more... go-fer...."

Bean heard the sharpness creep into the tone of his words and fell quiet. The silence followed them for several more hours, shadowing their steps down a steep rocky natural ramp. It lurked in the rough unhewn corners of tunnels and stone corridors that looked as though time had never so much as breathed on them, much less been touched by hammer or chisel. Bean reflected on things as they passed through this dim quiet world. He found himself wondering how deep beneath the ground they had traveled and how many miles lay between him and the Silver Dagger. Even the sight of Gort at this point, roaring orders at him and thumping him alongside the ear, would have been welcome. The quiet and darkness grated on his mind. Bean rubbed his eyes and began humming softly to himself, clicking his fingers, and doing anything he could to ward off the feeling of slowly going deaf and blind.

The air had grown warmer, becoming almost unbearably

hot by now and Bean heard a gurgling hissing noise that increased along with a strange red glow. Tight threads of fear wound around his chest, as his mind called up more visions of dragons curled up in lairs of molten lava. Fears quickly settled at the sight of a bed of hot springs nestled among red glowing crystals shaped like spear heads.

Steam drifted hazily through the tunnels as the path grew even more narrow and trickier. In the caldrons of stone, heavily crusted with deposits of minerals, murky water frothed and boiled furiously and a constant smell of sulphur burned Bean's nose. Flattened against the oily smooth walls, the boy edged his way along a writhing buckling serpent of a path, trying hard not to slip. A geyser suddenly burst straight up to the ceiling with a savage roar, not inches away from where Bean stood, startling him as a few bits of ceiling came tumbling and splashing down among the hot springs. Flecks of scalding water spattered across his face and clothes, stinging his bare skin, as he jerked his head away and squeezed his eyes shut tight. His foot slid a bit across the damp wet stone and he dug his fingernails into the wall behind him. He stopped, not wanting to move for a few minutes.

"Careful gofer, for the road is wet," said a voice. Bean opened one eye a tiny bit to see the Collector pressed against the wall, making his way towards the boy with a small deadly smile on his face, his eyes shining with poisonous mirth.

"But fear not for we are closer yet," he added. "It's through what remains of the forger's domain where fear became hope, but joy begat pain."

He prodded the boy onwards. Bean made himself move, stepping carefully over where the shelf of the path had crumbled down into the hot springs, while the waters gurgled, sputtered, and sizzled only a few inches away. Around a sharp curve, the mouth of a tunnel licked its stone lips with a dozen tongues of iron piping and the Collector motioned to it with a jerk of his head.

"Now through yon hole to the other side... And the blade I seek lies hidden inside," he commanded.

Bean inched his way carefully into the tunnel.

"Oh..." he muttered, looking around with wary eyes as the Collector came up beside him. A hand clamped onto his shoulder, pushing him forward. Bean could feel it trembling and the dull claws dug in painfully.

"Move along, boy, move along," he urged eagerly, barely able to keep his words from buzzing with hidden delight. "So close, so close is my song. Ah-ah... careful though with thy step..."

That same sickly-sweet odor of death brushed across Bean's nose. Here it lingered stronger and Bean felt his stomach turning again. People had died more recently here. A pile of huge rocks sprawled across the path. Bean shut his eyes and stepped quickly over the crushed remains of an unfortunate traveler whose chain-mail armor, however good it had been at warding off swords and arrows, hadn't stood a chance against several thousand tons of stone. He stared hard at the back of the Collector's head, pretending he didn't see the scattered helms, the bent and rusted weapons. Most importantly, he didn't want to see the cobblestones sunk down in strategic places across the floor and the cruel jagged lances of iron and chipped red crystal pinning the puppet-like bodies of more unfortunate adventurers to the walls of solid stone on either side of him. He ducked quickly as the red rock troll pushed a cunningly weighted pendulum blade out of his way and looked over his shoulder to watch the forge-blackened black blade swing back and forth gently across where they had walked. He tried not to notice the headless figure slumped over in the far corner, with its gray parchment-like skin peeling from pale-white bones and the dented helm at its feet, trailing long dusty locks of what might have once

102

been black hair.

"What... what happened here?" muttered Bean, rubbing his face. His words felt as though they wanted to lodge themselves in his throat and choke him. A door blown off its hinges by a powerful explosion lay twisted and dented in front of them and two crystals, one of which had been shattered, flanked the doorway. Bean turned to look back at the scene as the Collector approached the unbroken crystal. He heard a light-hearted twitter of chimes echo across the walls, as a strong white glow, like full moonlight, filled the room beyond the doorway and outlined the horrible tunnel into crisp shadows.

"Lurking through here were once many traps," said the Collector as a smug smile twitched the corners of his mouth. "Found them, I did... without a scratch. Yet many a gofer did not make it through. 'Tis sad, my boy... sad, but true."

He eyed Bean. The smile turned thoughtful as he murmured, "But you... you are different. Something unique. Someone the sword implored me to seek. Why would that be, gofer? Hm? What makes one such as you worthy of the attentions of the blade?" He added under his breath as he raised a quizzical eyebrow. He turned his ears expectantly, listening hard for the answer, but the song weaving through his thoughts continued on unbroken without a hint of purpose. As always, so many levels of understanding drifted just underneath the surface. However, the Collector felt quite confident he touched on them all as he turned and walked through the door into the paleness beyond it.

Bean stepped backwards absently.

"Oh... I see," he said, as he turned on his heels and emerged through the door. He lifted his head, his eyes traveled upwards and in that instant, the dark sickening closeness of the tunnels unveiled an ancient and splendid glory.

Words died for a moment. He could only stare and stare he did. Then his thoughts slowly resurrected themselves into one word, the only word that could possibly do justice to what he saw before him.

"Wow," he breathed. Then he said it again, "Wow!!!"

Strange Brews & Lonely Afternoons

Dark violet-edged clouds clustered together across the mid-morning sky and the air thickened with the smell of rain as the daylight dimmed. The sky growled ominously followed by the rose-tinted flicker of lightning.

A drop splattered into the dusty ground, with more drops rapidly following. Ravna glanced at the branches of the nearby trees as she hefted up a crate of bottled brews. The rain pecked playfully at the leaves, making them flutter and quiver like jittery butterflies. Lightning flashed boldly across the sky and a sudden clap of thunder shook the ground, rattling the bottles gently in their crates. Ravna winced and looked highly irritated.

"Lovely," she grumbled as the light dimmed. As if the storm had been heartened by her discouragement, the bottom promptly fell out of the sky.

"Wretched luck... and three more crates to go," she muttered to herself. She brushed the hair out of her eyes and trudged off across a ground already turning slick with mud, her skirt hem brushing through murky puddles. The thick dark muck swallowed her foot at one point, and she almost dropped the crate in her effort to pull her foot back out. Fortunately, she saved the crate but had to sacrifice her shoe in the process. She glared at the inviting doorway of the Silver Dagger.

"A pox... argh.... no, the blackclaw pox and... and the bloody eye flux... and a thousand curses from the grubby lips of... of every mule-drover from here to Cold Leaf be upon that walk back to the Dagger... do you hear me?!?! " She yelled to the sky and to no one in particular and limped back towards the Inn with the cold wetness soaking through her stocking.

Gort came to the door about the same time as Ravna. He leaned calmly on the doorframe, munching on a rosewine pear. Dark red pear juice trickled down his chin and stained the front of his already filthy shirt.

"Move it, ogre," Ravna grunted, her eyes dangerous behind a drape of stringy wet hair.

"Now Ravna, that not be nice," smirked Gort, spitting bits of pear everywhere as he spoke. "Where be those manners the Mistress of the Silver Dagger Inn be so known for?"

"Stuck out there in the rain in the be-cursed mud along with my shoe. So get out of the way before I drop this crate on your foot," said Ravna between tightly clenched teeth. Gort stepped back a bit to let her pass. Trailing muddy footprints across the floor, she marched to the storage shelves behind the bar and dropped the crate on top of the others with a satisfying loud clatter of bottles.

"Careful with them bottles, Mistress. That's Gort's hard-earned money what went into those drinks," the ogre cautioned her from the doorway. He grinned at Ravna's disgruntled expression.

"Hard-earned, my eye. I hope your pear is full of worms," the Mistress snorted and rubbed her nose as she walked past him.

Gort actually did see a fat green worm writhing around in the rosy heart of the pear when he took a second to look at it. However, he only shrugged and took another big hearty bite, worm and all. That sort of thing really didn't bother ogres.

"Now, now, thought we taught you better than that, Ravna," he teased as Ravna stormed out into the rain again. "Hurts my ol' heart to hear such talk. Maybe if you're nicer, I'll help you with the rest of those brews... after I'm done with my pear, of course."

Ravna splashed through the puddles and dug her shoe out of the mud. She tipped it over to pour out the water, smacked it against the sign post to get the mud off, and did a little hopping dance as she pulled it back on her foot. Then she whirled around; her hands balled up in fists and glared at Gort, her face twisted in fury.

"Look, you fat... filthy... slime-skinned toad!" she yelled at him. "You ought to... to be blessing the stars, the soil, and your lazy-rump ogre ancestors with your every breath that I choose to STAY in this cesspit of a forest. You, as well as every worthless drunk in Darkleaf!!! Now either help or shut your face!!!" She wiped her wet hair angrily from her eyes, smearing mud on her forehead. The look in her eyes could have set a tree on fire in the middle of an ice storm.

Gort took one last bite and tossed the pear over his shoulder. He rolled his eyes. "Oh, I've awakened the she-dragon, I have," he snorted, throwing his hands up in a mocking plea for mercy as he lumbered out into the rain. With hardly a grunt, he hefted up one crate on his shoulder and tucked another one under his arm, as Ravna picked up the last one.

"You be all touchy here of late, Mistress Ravna. Need to relax more," he said with a nod. "Bad tempers make for bad health, mm-hmm."

"You ought to be bed-ridden then, ogre," Ravna muttered

under her breath. Gort raised his brow.

"Mumble, mumble... talk like you've got a mouthful of pebbles. Speak up," he groused as they walked back through the door.

"I said, 'really? How fascinating...'" Ravna vigorously blew hair out of her face, as she sat her crate down and swept off with all the indignity of a half-drowned cat into the kitchen to find a wedge-bar.

Groggle sat by the open doorway, mournfully peeling a bucket full of potatoes sitting beside him. Occasionally he paused and looked up through the beaded curtain of water drizzling across the doorframe and down the path all misty and gray in the pouring rain. Then he would sigh heavily and go back to peeling. As he wiped a potato clean on his apron and dropped it into the pot of water on the other side of his feet, a dripping-wet Ravna came in and disappeared down the cellar stairs. Groggle heard her rummaging around in the tool bucket downstairs and from the clattering of falling rakes and shovels and the ringing of tossed hammers, Groggle guessed she wasn't so much as looking for something as venting her frustration on the tools. A few minutes later, she stormed back upstairs, knelt under the sink, and continued her search. Buckets, scrubbers, and various other items went skidding wildly across the floor. Finally she wriggled out from under the sink, looked around the kitchen, threw her hands up in exasperation, and promptly plopped down at the table nearby. She drummed her fingers against the table and glared at the wall.

"And, of course, I can't find the wedge-bar," she said stonily. Water dripped slowly from her, making little puddles on the kitchen floor. Her lower lip trembled from the damp cold.

Groggle set his knife aside and quietly lumbered out of the kitchen, sliding the scattered items with his foot back under the sink on his way. When he came back, he had several blankets and silently draped them over Ravna.

"Now, now, Ravna," he said. "Not all that bad."

"Yes, it is. If I don't have a wedge-bar, I can't open those crates of leaf brew and I won't have anything to hit Gort with," Ravna muttered, her eyes still on the wall as she pulled the blankets closer around her. Groggle glanced wearily up at the ceiling, wrinkling his brow. He shook his head, went to the cabinet and took out a large mug, as well as a few bags of fragrant herbs.

"Ah, don't worry. Just leave the crates for Siv. Some catmint tea, maybe?" he said.

"Maybe," Ravna replied, resting her chin in her hand. Groggle measured out half a cup of the dried pale-green leaves and broken stems into the mug, as well as a few peppermint leaves and chamomile flowers. Then he walked over to the stove to retrieve a kettle of water he had set there earlier. He carefully poured the boiling water over the mixture and as it steeped and cooled a bit, he looked thoughtfully over his bags of herbs, glanced over at Ravna, and then discreetly pulled a dried rather ugly-looking root out of one bag. When he broke a bit off, a sharp bracing sweet smell filled the air.

He crushed it into powder in his hand and sprinkled it in the tea before stirring it up and putting the bags away again.

"Here you are, drink it up. Warm the soul and bones it will," he nodded as he brought the fragrant tea over to the table. Ravna cupped the mug in her hand and sniffed it thoughtfully. She looked sideways at Groggle.

"No rat dandruff for flavoring?" she asked, warily.

"No rat anything, I promise you. Catmint, a few tea-herbs... all it be."

A faint smile traveled across her face. She sipped delicately from the mug and it did taste so good, almost intoxicating. She felt the chill, the frustration, and the anger slipping away in the comfortable warmth of the hot tea.

"Thank you, Groggle."

"Eh... you're welcome," said Groggle in a distracted sort of way as he picked up a tray of bones and leftovers sitting on the chopping block and went to dump them in the waste-barrel by the door. A deep silence filled the kitchen, broken only by the mutter of thunder and the drumming rain from the open door.

Ravna ran her finger along the rim of the mug. "Groggle... are you all right?" she asked finally, as the ogre settled himself down by his potatoes and started peeling again. "Groggle?" she repeated gently.

"Huh? Oh... all right? Yes... yes, why wouldn't I be?" mumbled Groggle. "Fine I am..." He paused and glanced through the door again.

"Just fine..." he added, even though his sad eyes and frown told a different story.

Ravna rubbed her hair dry with the blanket and let it drape down over her shoulders, as she turned in her chair to look at the old ogre.

"Siv will find the Bean, Groggle," she said. "You know he will."

"Eh? Bean? Ahh..." Groggle scratched his rough-skinned neck and sighed. "Wasn't... wasn't even thinking about the lad. 'Course Siv will find him... of course he will." He glanced down at the potatoes and tapped his knife blade restlessly on the edge of the bucket. "But still my fault," he murmured. "Still my fault. Shrooms..."

Tap-tap-tap went the knife. Then with a clang, Groggle dropped the knife on the floor and slowly stood up again. He stared out the back door, rubbing his hand across his broad chest with a distant look in his eyes.

"Groggle?"

The ogre's shoulders slumped and his head abruptly dropped. Then without a word or a glance, he walked out into the driving rain. Ravna raised her eyebrows, got up from the table, and went to the door. "Groggle!!!" she called sharply and then in a gentler voice, "Groggle... where are you go-ing?"

He turned around and looked blearily back at her as the pounding rain made a fine aura of mist across his

broad shoulders and head and trickled in narrow streams from his hands. He blinked water from his eyes and his ears twitched a bit.

"Need some more shrooms," he sighed in a gloomy voice as he jerked his head in the direction of the path. Ravna leaned against the doorframe and pulled the blankets closer around her.

"Groggle. Please stay," she finally said.

Groggle cleared his throat, sniffed reflectively, ran his hand over his face, and looked back over his shoulder at the path again.

"Watch those kettles on the stove for ol' Groggle. I'll... I'll be back soon," he said and with a nod, turned away and set off again, splashing and squelching through mud puddles. Ravna watched him becoming a dim gray blur on the rise of the path before he disappeared entirely and nothing could be seen but the sheeting rain and the dark outlines of the fence and the trees. A bird called somewhere out in the rain, a clear crisp call like the knocking of hollow bones. A chill hanging in the air made Ravna rub her arms and shiver. She found herself musing, wondering how Siv must be faring in this weather.

Abruptly a hissing bubbling noise came from the stove as one of the kettles threatened to boil dry. Ravna sighed deeply, feeling as gray and washed out as the scenery outside, and went to go tend to the stove as Groggle had asked her to.

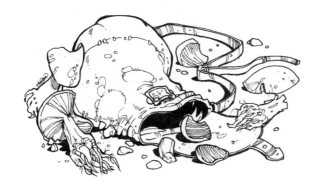

the Forestwalker

The forest of Darkleaf had a voice that sang, whispered, shouted, and growled. It spoke to those who bothered taking the time to listen. For those who wouldn't listen however, the forest could be indifferent at its kindest and ruthless at its cruelest. Darkleaf had no patience for slow learners.

Siv knew all this. Forestwalker had not been a title granted idly to him, so he listened as he walked through the woods in the pouring rain and heard many things that casual travelers often missed. He listened to the contented peeping of small frogs and the drops of rain striking the leaves and falling into puddles. He listened to the slosh of the mud and water underneath his feet, the rustling of some small animal running through the underbrush to find shelter, and the scrape of branches against each other as the wind keened through them like a lost soul. Mostly though he listened to the thoughts inside his own head, thoughts that clip-clopped across cobblestone streets and murmured behind closed doors, old friends that had been his only company on too many cold nights as he stood breathless in the shadows and waited for footsteps.

Every sound, no matter how small or insignificant is worthy of acknowledgment. Siv heard those familiar words spoken softly again within his mind. Far behind him, the rain beat down on a quiet glen, empty save for a limp bag lying among scattered dargle shrooms and unanswered questions.

Siv intended to find answers, but the trail he followed had grown increasingly fragile and more... tangled, but not because the rain had washed away telltale tracks or signs. He followed a trail of perceptions that constantly shifted and redefined themselves before his mind could completely process what they were. Perhaps, as he walked, he heard a faint sound like that of thousands of tiny crystals shattering and reassembling themselves. Then in another couple of steps, he caught a whiff of ice on a rusted and forgotten blade or perhaps, in the outside edges of his vision, his surroundings would shimmer briefly like illuminated vapors. There lay the difficulty of following such a trail. In the wake of his quarry he felt as if he waded neck-deep through sour oil-laced wine, for the tainted air clung to his skin and made the hairs raise on his arms and the back of his neck. To add to his general discomfort, Siv also kept running into spots where the trail flittered off into different directions, tempting him away with invisible threads, spun of sudden hopes and gossamer light that disintegrated into nothing after a couple of strides into the undergrowth.

He knew all these tricks. He recognized the pine branch being swept across footprints, the false sensations and impressions designed to confuse and mask the truth. Unfortunately, they worked all too well. Knowing the illusions didn't change their effects or the uneasy truth of a weaver's presence in Darkleaf and an uncommonly powerful one at that. This only bothered Siv more because it all boiled down to a single question: why?

Siv wiped his face on his sleeve, as he stepped off into a shallow trench brimming with murky water. He rested his hand on the mossy trunk of a huge fallen tree, ducked beneath it, and pushed aside a dripping curtain of tattered vines. As he sloshed onward, he absently noted the hollow clicking of a sibyl bird and looked up to see it perched on the jutting twig of a hawthorn bush, its milky blue eyes half-closed as it enjoyed the rain. It lifted up its white beak and its tiny red throat throbbed as it called again, tossing the fortune-bones that told one's destiny, or so the old superstitious farmers and merchants of Darkleaf always claimed.

> *"...Then rode he onward through the darkling wood*
> *Ride e'er proud, ye sons of the north*
> *He wept and cursed, seeing death would not wait*
> *As he heard the sibyl bird call out his fate*
> *Then spear in his hand, he cried for their blood*
> *Ride e'er proud, ye sons of the north..."*

Siv hummed under his breath, the fragments of the old ballad piecing themselves together from dim memories. "Odd how a simple call from a drab little bird could dust off one's mind like that," he thought. When he tried to recall the rest of the song though, he only drew a blank. He sighed and suddenly felt a lot older.

He waded out onto higher ground again, took a moment to knock mud from his boots, and kept on walking. His brows furrowed in concentration as he struggled to follow the signs through the woods that no ordinary huntsman could ever imagine. He pondered, and not without a touch of ruefulness, if he had been mistaken all those years ago, for not making more of an effort to understand the complexities of weaver society and the weaver's mind. After all, there had been opportunities once, opportunities that he easily could have turned to his advantage without having gone in over his head. In the light of better understanding, the events might have been changed.

"And if so, either way you certainly wouldn't be here now in Darkleaf," came the quick thought. As it always did, those same questions came back to nag him. "Where would those choices have taken you, Siv? Would you still be the same man you are now?"

"Would I?"

He concluded that some questions simply had no answers. That was the sorrow of it all, but in a strange sort of way, not knowing could also be a blessing. Perhaps he could have anticipated things better had he chosen his path differently. Perhaps everything he understood now in retrospect could have been realized in those critical moments of long ago. Still, somewhere deep within White Hall stood a wall of stained glass, lit by candle glow, and etched with a thousand faceless forgotten names of those who made their choices and never had the chance to look back or wonder why. Slodging through mud and muck chasing after a lost little boy couldn't be considered the best of circumstances in any light, but at least this had been a choice Siv felt he could live with. Better to be a forgotten name in glass than to be remembered in stone for all the wrong reasons.

He had been going steadily uphill now for sometime and here the bones of Darkleaf lay exposed among the ancient trees. Tall and stately walls of broken stones thrust up from the thin earth and broad overhangs partly shadowed the paths. Siv took a moment to rest under one of these stone eaves. He fished around in his haversack and pulled out a few shreds of dried sloth-meat, and as he chewed thoughtfully on his meager meal, he silently thanked Ravna for her sweet and stubborn ways. She had come a long way from the bitter young woman wrapped in tatters who had come up to the door of the Inn not so long ago, looking for shelter from the cold winter night. As he sat and watched the rain dripping down outside of his shelter, Siv sincerely hoped that the fierce fire within her that had sustained her so well through her personal tragedies and her daily difficulties would never fade. Ravna never knew how much she meant to those of the Silver Dagger, or that Siv counted her as the dearest of friends.

He had pulled out his pipe by now, contemplating a brief smoke before moving on, when out of the corner of his eye something flickered, a flash of unnatural color among the misty gray of the pounding rain and the dark muted patchwork of browns and greens. Siv immediately came to attention and as he did, his ears told him something else was wrong. Except for the rain, which thrummed down steadily, and the occasional growl of thunder, Darkleaf had fallen silent. The woods had grown watchful and guarded and to Siv it was a clear signal to do likewise.

He moved carefully out from beneath the rock and continued along his way, slipping easily in and out between the shadows of the rocks and the trees. The path of the weave led him higher, until at the rise of the path he abruptly veered off into the concealing undergrowth. Careful now to not even break a twig recklessly beneath his feet or slosh too loudly in and out of the puddles, Siv continued to keep both eyes and ears open and one hand ready to draw his sword as he traveled further into the woods.

Then he saw it.

Siv stopped dead in his tracks. He knelt down at the broad face of the rock before him, twisted and cracked from the aggressive roots of a nearby elm, and stared at what lay in pieces in front of it like a shattered black thorn. He carefully reached out a hand and gathered it together. He stood up and studied what lay in his hands.

An arrow. A black arrow, fletched with ragged and dull red feathers with a barbed head of forge-blackened iron.

Goblins...

Siv's dark eyes narrowed. The drumming rain soaking into his clothes and skin seemed to have gotten a lot colder.

As he stood there, he suddenly became sharply aware of the remains of the weave, decaying rapidly around him, like a tapestry

unraveling into floating particles of dust and light, an urgent warning he dared not ignore. He drew out his sword as he glanced behind at the path only a few strides away

"And they're close," he thought to himself. "Blast…"

He took off deeper into the woods; heading for the higher ground, as lightning ripped across the sky above his head and the ground beneath his feet shuddered at the answering peal of thunder. The trail had gone cold, but a more pressing task had been laid before him.

A bristling host of goblins moved steadily through the heart of Darkleaf, trudging across the slick muddy path. Siv wiped the rain from his eyes as he lay motionless on the broad face of the ridge and watched their passage far below him. Behind his still expression, his thoughts churned, the rain hammering against his back. His fingers tapped thoughtfully against the blade of his sword lying beside him for a moment before he curled his hand around the leather hilt once again. He propped himself up on his elbow and slid backwards across the ridge, keeping his head low.

"And what would you be doing thus armed and so deep here in the forest, my goblin friends? The likes of that hasn't been seen in quite a few generations," Siv murmured under his breath, as he climbed down the rock face, jumped lightly off near the bottom, and landed with a soft grunt on the ground.

Scooping up handfuls of dark mud, he rubbed it into his white hair, over his face, and into his clothes. The less obvious he made himself against the background of the forest, the more secure he felt. From another pocket, he took out several dark waxbulb roots, crushed them, and quickly rubbed them across his sword, blackening the blade to prevent giving himself away with an accidental flash of metal. Satisfied with his appearance he set off to shadow the goblins.

Tapping into every source of forest-skill and stealth he had, Siv crept along quietly on the outskirts of the main path, dogging the heels of the goblin regiment. He got close enough at times to catch glimpses of the spearheads of carved palestone and black iron and the glint of green-tinged bronze rivets and bronze wire grips against dark red wood. As he moved unseen through the woods, his heart quickened its pace and his mind cleared.

Despite the seriousness of the situation, an old familiar exhilaration he thought long gone stagnant from years behind a bar began to stir up the dull blood within him. He moved off in a different direction intending to head them off and get as close a look at them as he dared. A few minutes later found Siv lying on his stomach in a shallow ditch beneath the concealing shadows of several low bushes, watching the goblins passing by so closely he could have reached out and touched them. He could see the water beading up against the brown slickness of their oilcloth cloaks, hear the mud squelching between their rag-wrapped feet and as the cloaks rippled past him, he noticed the dull glint of armor beneath the oilcloth. Siv took a grim sort of satisfaction in being so invisible.

Suddenly every instinct in him compelled him to be still as, what he had first thought to be a pack-beast of some sort, padded into view. Shreds of tattered gray rags and crude amulets swung and clicked gently against each other as the creature moved with a strange half-beast half-human gait, loping easily along on four legs or partly upright and dragging its front claws along on the muddy ground. A filthy stained muzzle of leather and bone covered its mouth and its head bobbed back and forth as it glanced around. As it neared Siv, he saw blood flecked across its head and claws and he saw, too, that the steady movement of its head seemed more methodical than that of a mere animal whiffing at the air.

It grew still, suddenly stopping in its tracks, as it observed its surroundings. Siv held his breath. He could feel the creature listening and saw a long thin thread of red-tinged saliva dripping from the corners of the muzzle as it breathed noisily. In those heavy-lidded

green eyes, that seemed far too human for comfort, Siv saw a shine of intelligence he liked even less. One saw that sort of dull gleam in the eyes of a man calmly raising a knife to his own throat or in the eyes of a woman who had just killed her own child. It told Siv that the knowledge behind those soul-less eyes waded through the depths of desperation, hand-in-hand with self-destruction, and it did so with a gladness that finalized the full horror of it all.

Finally the creature's claws tightened as goblins trudged past it. Those eyes, resting their level murderous gaze over Siv's hiding spot, slitted as it turned its head away and continued on, scratching at the amulets around its neck with a deliberately casual sort of malice. One sudden violent swipe of those long black nails, that gesture seemed to say, and it really wouldn't matter who became the prey, be it friend or foe, goblin or human.

Siv didn't move for several minutes after the last of the goblins had passed him by. He felt the chill of the rain seeping into his legs and arms, but he far preferred that to the chill that crept up his backbone and twisted in his gut as his mind processed what he had seen.

The word, "gren-el," reared its ugly head out of the depths of his thoughts. He wanted to shrug it away, to brush off the stories of elves that so willingly embraced this irreversible madness as just that, folklore and tales to frighten children with. He struggled to fit that creature within the barrier of the animal kingdom, instead of letting himself believe that the nature of intelligent beings, such as elves or humans could also include the dark and twisted desires that had birthed such an abomination.

"Yet how easily words of hatred and scorn had fallen from fair and smiling lips," came the silent comment. "How voices, as gentle and kind as a spring breeze, had brought suffering. You've seen it and heard it all too many times before. Lies do not become a man such as yourself, Siv."

Siv smiled grimly to himself as he slid back from the road

and set off after the goblins again. "Especially self-deluding lies," he added silently.

The keen awareness of that creature, he admitted, had been a bit too close for comfort. If it hadn't actually seen him (and he hoped that very much) Siv still couldn't shake the feeling that only a few minutes longer would have changed all that, although whether that was due to animal instincts or something else, he didn't want to speculate about right now. More important now was to hold pace with those wretched goblins. He kept as reasonable a distance behind them as he could manage, tracking them through the forest, down into ravines flooded with water, and over hills where the going went even rougher as he was forced to make his way slowly up steep inclines, slick and treacherous with mud.

Finally, as he fought through a wall of thick underbrush coming down the opposite side of a particularly tall hill, the trees thinned out into a wide vale sheltered all around by tall conifers and twisted oaks. Siv's eyes widened and he raised his eyebrow slightly.

"By the broken moon..." he breathed as he knelt behind a root in the shadow of a looming oak.

"Darkness was here first in the world before anything else and it is here still, hidden and deceptive. Sometimes one must have to light a candle and show it for what it really is." The words of his old elvish friend seemed more appropriate than ever as he stared at the huge untidy bivouac that lay sprawled out before him like a vast hornet's nest. Tents and crude watchtowers surrounded hastily constructed stockades and barriers of dead thorn-bushes. This wasn't just a stray raiding party down from the mountains. Here, deep in the heart of the forest, an army gathered itself, organized as he had never before thought possible under ordinary goblin leadership. Darkleaf spoke to those who knew how to listen, but unfortunately, the forest also kept some very nasty secrets.

Siv traveled the outer boundary of the campsite several times under the cover of the trees, listening, making observations, and keeping invisible. He noted the weakest spots in the overall organization of the encampment and decided to take a calculated risk. At the west end where the security appeared to be the most relaxed and the barriers were the most haphazardly constructed, Siv patiently bided his time studying the sentries and their routine up in the watchtower closest to where he crouched hidden in the woods. At the changing of the guard, Siv took advantage of their temporary inattention to their duties and darted towards the stockade, positioning himself carefully just beneath their line of vision. He crept quickly along, his back scraping against the rough wood and rounded the corner of the stockade. When he reached the barrier of thorn bushes lining the row of tents, it was then just a matter of forcing the vicious prickly branches back with the blade of his sword to allow himself a suitable opening to slip through.

Here he soon discovered the pack beasts standing hobbled and corralled, great snub-nosed nubbly skinned alytas that moved around in their pens a bit and grunted irritably at his sudden appearance but otherwise took little notice of him. Siv wiped his sword clean with his shirt sleeve, sheathed it, and stuck close to the living quarters of the alyta drivers, weaving skillfully in and out of the shadows until he came to exactly the stroke of luck he needed to continue.

A lone soldier had ducked into a sheltered alley between the tents to catch a quiet moment alone to himself and to also enjoy a bit of vhagua-root, a mildly addictive but foul-smelling narcotic which formed a popular vice among the goblins. The soldier packed the crumbled root into the corner of his jaw, licked a peeled twig and ran it around the rim of a pottery jar full of soursalt to stick back in his mouth to cut the sharpness of the bitter root.

He didn't notice who came up behind him until it was too late to matter. Abruptly, the pot thudded to the ground and the twig clattered across it as the yellow soursalt spilled across the wet ground.

Rag-wrapped feet scrabbled desperately in the mud and then a muffled snap brought silence.

A while later, a tall figure draped in an oilcloth cloak emerged from the shelter of the tents and moved mutely through the midst of the goblin camp. No one paid the man much attention, a hundred other human soldiers like him walked among the goblins around the encampment. Behind a couple of feed barrels near the pens, the rain pounded down on a filthy alyta blanket partially covering a still form.

The garrison buzzed with activity, even more so since the arrival of the latest raiding party. Those involved talked casually of their deeds, as well as other matters, to fellow soldiers as they stood clustered around tents or squatted beneath whatever shelter was available.

"...Burned it to the ground, we did, yes. More vittles for the troops... fresh meat, oh yes," grunted one with a dismal expression on his face, holding out his hand and letting the rain stream through it. "Faugh! Filthy weather, this," his fellows solemnly nodded their agreement to both comments.

"Vengeance comes, so says the Beast King, heh," added one, a younger goblin with a gleeful smirk on his ugly face. "Our right to take it all back. No more cold mountains, no more scratchin' and sniffin' about for vittles. Darkleaf be our rosy apple, ripe for the pluckin'." More hearty agreements and nods followed this comment. The first goblin waved his hand dismissively.

"Wise our Beast King, yes. Wiser he'd be to spit that pig-commander though." He snorted. "Be done with the fat Badger, says I. Feed 'im to the troops. Won't need to eat for months afterwards." He cackled loudly at his own joke and a couple of others joined him in uneasy laughter.

"Narkle thought like that and Narkle hangs now on the stone walls of Grimnorp. The Badger's been right over and over. He and the Beast King... almost one mind and one power, they be, an' we eats better under them than under the old azhlars," pointed out one of his companions who hadn't joined in the joke. "Not organized before, not like now. Told us, they both did, that the woodsfolk and farmers weren't even prepared. Be easy as it was for our fathers before us, said the Badger."

"Hah! Told you that also," retorted the goblin, jabbing a fingernail at him. "Full of mule-spit he is..."

"Fights good, though, for a human,"

"Fought good without him, we did. Oh yes... cut 'em down like strawgrass," answered the goblin and thumped his chest, as he swelled with self-importance. "The forest belongs to us..."

The cloaked man walked silently past the goblins as they continued arguing. As well as that disturbingly confident last comment, Siv noted the names of Badger and Beast King and stored them away for future pondering.

A goblin alyta driver and two unsavory-looking human soldiers stood warming themselves by one of several forges as the weather grew wetter and colder. Nearby a sweating blacksmith, also human, folded and shaped a glowing red metal spearhead against an anvil. Sparks jumped into the air with every blow of his hammer, dying with little hisses when they hit the soaked ground. Smelters, both goblin and human, melted iron ore in huge caldrons in a partly sheltered courtyard back behind the forge, while others shoveled fuel into the forge-fires and stacked into wicker baskets, newly made spearheads, arrowheads, and swords waiting to be finished.

"...And you still think the Badger is the better leader?" one of the human soldiers asked his companion.

"Better than what we had before," admitted the other man. "Look how far we have gotten with him on our side. We would have never taken Long Creek and Pale Leaf, otherwise."

"You may be right there, friend," nodded the first soldier. "Since we've hooked up with these shackle-beaters, times have been good." His voice lowered as he added, "The Badger's a pig of a leader though. Filthy creature."

"Must be why the goblins think so highly of him, then," his friend answered with a broad grin and they both chuckled. The comments however didn't escape the sharp ears of the alyta driver, who turned at the laughter and glared hatefully at the two soldiers.

"We wins under the Badger, oh yes. They all fear us," he sneered. "Needn't talk so of the Badger, else he feed you to the elf-beasts like he did the folk of the last town." The men exchanged significant glances with one another.

"Haven't you got an alyta pen to muck out or something?" said one with a disdainful expression on his face. "You needn't talk in such a disrespectful tone of voice to your betters, shackle-beater, or I'll report you."

"Could also tell the Badger what you jus' said... human," retorted the goblin and both the soldiers smirked.

"And what did I just say? I can't seem to recall now," said the first man and prodded the goblin hard between the shoulder blades with the butt of his spear. "You'd get in quite a bit of trouble telling lies about those who outrank you. I'm willing to bet a good honest human soldier would be believed over a dirty goblin who smells of alyta dung. Get along with you now, pointy-ears."

The goblin snarled a scathing curse at the man in his own language and for a tense moment he looked as though he would lunge at the soldier. The man swiftly flipped his spear and lowered it in a gesture of warning. Then, oddly enough, the goblin seemed to reconsider his action and stepped back, as he grinned coldly at the soldier.

"Talk big for a man, you do," he remarked. "Badger be lucky now to have us and the gren-els... but you wait... one day they go. Better to take your chances with the elf-beasts then, human." He spat on the spearhead and walked off as more goblins approached. Both soldiers hardly seemed bothered by the threat and went back to talking.

"Hoy, Worm-Eye!" called the blacksmith cheerfully to one of the passing goblins, as he dropped his hammer and wiped his filthy face with his leather apron. "Back from your little picnic in Darkleaf, I see." The goblin waved a lethargic hand in the blacksmith's direction. "Made a few farmer's brats squeal, did you? Must've been music to your pointy little ears. Pity I missed seeing it!" He chuckled, as he picked up the glowing red spearhead with his tongs and doused it in the cooling-bucket with a loud hiss and cloud of steam. A hideous grin spread across Worm-Eye's face. He gave an amiable sort of nod to the man as he passed him, but when he turned his head, the smile quickly changed into a look of disgust. He made an acidic comment obviously concerning the blacksmith in his own tongue to his companions, and a couple of the goblins snickered nastily.

Beneath the shadowed hood, the corner of Siv's mouth twitched slightly and his hands clenched. He quickened his pace to take him as far as possible from the grinning goblins and the blacksmith with his vile jokes.

Beneath a dripping leather tarp outside of another tent, fletchers sat around a crackling fire, engaged in the task of whittling, sanding, and painting arrow shafts black. A pot of crimson dye seethed on the fire as one goblin with red-stained hands dumped a sack of feathers into it and stirred them around with a stick. Freshly dyed feathers air-dried on a covered frame nearby. Siv stood with his back to another fire nearby under the pretense of warming himself and listened to their conversations.

"...elfs on the other side of the river. Take them before the second snows, says I," remarked one, as he scooped up a handful of wood shavings up at his feet and tossed them into the fire.

"Powerful elfs they be, though... be a bad battle, yes," said another.

"Faugh! Elfs will never walk these woods again, so says the Beast King," said a third goblin, splitting up a large slab of yellow poplar wood into smaller rodlets with a hammer and several wedges. "Gots the gren-els on our side, yes. Elf-cousins be rippin' the throats out of their wood-kindred. We don't fear elfs."

"Oh, hate those gren-els... evil, evil beasts they are," murmured another whittler, as he stacked his finished work by his feet.

"Not far from Heartleaf, now. The crow-eyes and runners brought back news, this morning. Crow-eyes says all well-stocked, yes; a nice, plump hen of a town. Soon we wring its neck, heh-heh," snickered a goblin sitting beside him as he painted the arrow-shaft. "Badger will be happy, yes, oh yes..."

"Yet the Beast King wants it. Wants the whole forest to 'izelf."

"Flay 'im and be done with the Beast King and his pet badger. A fool he is... muttering and moaning about lost relics and old stones," growled the feather-dyer suddenly as he stirred his cauldron. "Raskar Crittooth be the leader for us. With him, we win... with him we eats the fresh meat. Fools we were to close our mouths and look away while the Beast King took our pride and our swords and made pampered pets of our old azhlars. But Crittooth... now there be the goblin prince for us, yes. He be cunning, he remembers his pride...

he'll bring us back to our glory days afore you milk-soppers can kiss another toe!"

A thoughtful silence followed this declaration. The goblins looked sideways at each other. Eyes narrowed suspiciously and then they all started arguing and contending at once. The quarrel quickly became louder and more heated. Bowls of black paint clattered on their sides and spilled, as a couple of the goblins got up to face off against the dyer, who narrowed his eyes, bared his teeth, and brandished his stick in one threatening red-stained hand. Other soldiers attracted by the commotion began gathering around to watch and Siv quietly slipped away from the fire, as behind him old tribal grudges and hostilities flamed up into violence.

He passed a group of soldiers struggling with and shrilly cursing a particularly uncooperative pack-beast while a goblin balanced himself on the harness and cried, "Taah! Hup-hup!" as he lay about mercilessly on the animals' flanks with a barbed urging-flail and cut deep scores into the mottled hide. Another couple of goblins stood outside of a tent. One had opened a dark-stained bag, bragging of his raiding-party's accomplishments as someone might brag of a particularly successful hunting trip.

"...stuck a bit but a knife took care of it, yes... a pretty gold wristlet... hang all my trophies up to dry once this pig-spittle rain stops... not quite dead when I started to cut off the hand..."

The goblin chattered away as he rummaged around in the bag. Siv caught a faint sickly-sweet odor of decay and turned his face aside as he walked by. The idea of seeing that filthy creature's trophies sickened him. This whole wretched cesspool, filled with such scum of the earth as goblins and beasts, which called themselves men, sickened him as nothing had before.

Then Siv smiled coldly to himself beneath his hood as memories of heated pursuits down narrow mountain paths and old battles waged long ago against raiding goblins came back in his mind. Beasts they all were indeed and he prided himself in being a skilled hunts-man. He would see them flushed out of their foul nest and run to earth before much longer. Only a few tasks more, he thought. He had to satisfy himself with knowing he had enough information to decide his next course of actions and he had to exhaust every pos-sible lead concerning the fate of Bean. The hope of finding survivors among these animals grew dimmer all the time, especially since Siv knew their brutal ways all too well. However, even as jaded to the world as he considered himself, some conclusions Siv found he simply couldn't bring himself to consider, until he knew them to be, beyond any doubt, the harsh truth. Especially when it involved a little boy.

He made his way into the winding alleys behind the tents, walking past haphazard piles of barrels and jugs, until the noise and bustle grew faint behind him. The wind picked up, wailing eerily as it blew past him and made the cloth walls surrounding him flap fit-fully as he stopped at a likely looking tent. Glancing around to make sure that no one saw him, he listened carefully for a moment before he drew out his sword once more, knelt down on the cold churned mud, lifted up a corner of the tent, and slid lightly into the darkness beyond it.

Over by the animal pens, an alyta driver broke open a barrel of feed and in the process happened to notice one of the pack-beasts' blankets thrown carelessly behind the feed barrels. He grumbled to himself about the thoughtlessness of the soldiers, since unlike some of his fellow drivers, he did actually care for his beasts. He began pulling out the barrels to try and see if he could reach it, while the rain continued sheeting down over the campsite and lightning briefly whitened the sky.

the Song's Call

Faces gazed down on the Bean, ancient faces, wise and solemn. Their dark eyes of crystal slowly illuminated into shining golden life at the coaxing of the chimes drifting up into the air like the sparks from a fire. Light and music filled the vast chamber as crystals and cunningly placed mirrors inset in the stone walls and ceiling banished the shadows. The gaze of those empty golden eyes in the still faces of white stone was something that Bean knew would haunt him for the rest of his life.

He and the Collector stood on a floor of highly polished inlaid marble, yellow and badly mottled now from age and damp, that sometime in the distant past had once been pure white. They faced a stone facade of four column statues that towered over the both of them. Immense statues of men or perhaps elves, Bean couldn't be sure from where he stood, but all were dressed in what definitely looked like armor. As he studied them, he realized something else; the face of the farthest statue from where he stood had been almost completely destroyed. Somehow the sight of the raw scarred rock instead of the calm and noble visage that should have been there bothered Bean deeply. He rubbed the prickles from the back of his neck and followed the Collector towards the foot of the columns.

In the wall before them gaped a hole that looked as though the same force that had blown the door open had also done its job here with devastating effectiveness. Its charred jagged edges marred the smooth whiteness of the rock. The Collector shrugged the pack off of his shoulders, opened it, and rummaged around inside of it. Unsure of what to expect next, Bean stared down at his toes and his eyes traced the intricate patterns carved in the stones beneath his feet. He could hear the Collector humming eagerly to himself.

" So... soon... the blade at last. Its song finally within my grasp." He said under his breath. "And the lovely sword, mine all mine, power to wield, power sublime..."

He pulled out a coil of rope and held out the end to Bean. "Gather your wits and your rope, boy," he ordered, as he gestured to the opening. "Here is where we part ways."

Bean moved closer with a doubtful frown on his face. He leaned down and peered through the hole.

"In there?" he asked.

The Collector nodded and the boy swallowed hard. "But..." he started.

"No buts... no hesitation. Hurry, you go now," snapped the Collector.

"It's... it's so dark," whispered Bean as his head sunk down a little further between his shoulders. He could smell the stale air in the pitch-blackness beyond the hole.

The Collector glared at the boy with a sneer of absolute disdain crossing his face.

"'Dark' say you, lad?"

he mocked. "To what does that profit me?" He straightened himself up slightly and put out a hand to steady himself. He bared his teeth in a snarl and furious impatience distorted his features as his hand tightened into a ball.

"Fail... HERE and NO NEED have I for THEE!!!" he roared, abruptly smacking the side of his fist against the stone. The boy shrank away from the sudden mad outburst. He heard the short quick breaths of rage shuddering between the creature's teeth and saw the wild impatient gleam in his eye, as the Collector thrust his twisted face into the boy's vision once more.

"Whine if you will of darkness and fear. I'll see thy bones within thee seared and send thy little simpering soul to whine and moan in the darkness below!!!" he grated. The end of the rope struck the boy sharply across his face and the Collector's eyes slitted.

"Now... take the rope," he ordered, holding it out to him.

Bean rubbed the side of his face, feeling the welt beneath his fingers.

"...Okay..." he said in a small voice and tried not to look at the Collector as he obeyed his order.

He tied the rope as tightly as he could around his waist, as per the Collector's muttered instructions, and knelt down to peer into the hole again. He swallowed hard and carefully rested his hands against the rough edges of the broken rock. Ducking his head, he slipped inside a narrow and low-ceilinged passage of roughly laid stone. He pushed aside stones, as best as he could and gingerly crawled over jagged piles of rubble that cut and bruised his hands and knees.

"One more thing, gofer..." came the Collector's low voice from outside of the hole. Bean turned his head and looked back at the shadowed face staring at him with wild shining eyes.

"What is it?" Bean asked.

The Collector drew a claw across his throat and smiled coldly.

"Don't cheat me," he murmured.

Bean's mouth felt painfully dry. He coughed and gave a quick nod before he turned his attention back to the tunnel and the darkness ahead of him. He squeezed his eyes shut and made his way carefully along on his hands and knees.

"I won't... I won't..." he whispered to himself.

He brushed wispy spider webs out of his way as he crawled along and bit his bottom lip when something ticklish and too alive for his comfort landed on the back of his hand. He swatted it quickly away and crawled faster, not daring to open his eyes. Further down the tunnel the ground abruptly vanished under his hand and he tumbled forward into the darkness with a gasp. His fall jerked to a quick halt and he swung wildly for a moment, his arms and legs waving in terror, vainly trying to find some sort of hold somewhere. His forehead struck rock jutting out from somewhere.

"Yowch!" he yelped, his voice echoing in the blackness. He clutched his scraped forehead with one hand and hissed between his teeth in pain, as his other hand waved around for the rock and found it again. He steadied himself against it and as he turned gently in the air, he tried reaching gingerly down with his foot, feeling for any kind of support. Afraid of finding himself suspended miles above a deep chasm, he felt great relief to realize that the solid floor lay only a few inches further below his feet. He wriggled down lower along the rope until he could stand and tugged on it a bit to signal for some slack. As the rope coiled around his feet he put his hand up again to keep himself from striking his head against the rock and felt his way down a gently sloping passage covered in scree. Thankfully he had more room to stand up, but the mess of loose rocks and sand beneath his feet made the going tricky.

Bean tripped, stumbled, and slid his way ever downwards, waving his hands ahead of his face to keep from bumping into anything. Finally the slope let up onto level ground again. The ceiling started getting lower and he put one hand up on it and crouched

down slightly as he walked blind in the blackness with his other hand held straight in front of him. Before long his fingers brushed against a stone wall directly in front of him and after feeling around in the darkness, Bean quickly discovered the edges of another opening about shoulder-high from the floor. He hoisted himself up and through it.

Bean dropped down into another corridor, a larger one. He fumbled around in the darkness and his hand touched something smooth and cold, which grew suddenly warm as a musical drone filled the air. Light illuminated his surroundings as a line of large crystals lit up along the side the walls of the tunnel. Bean realized his hand had touched one of these crystals, but instead of soft golden light, these crystals gave off a harsh blue glow edged in crisp brilliant white. His hand slid off of the crystal and touched the stone palm of a very realistically carved hand. Bean looked down and his face grew thoughtful. He spread his fingers gently over the cool fingers of the stone hand. Four, exactly the same as his own.

More carvings stared at him from the walls, thrown into hard relief by the bright light, images Bean didn't understand at all. Times of war and times of peace told their silent stories, as they unfolded across the lifeless stone. He assumed that the lines of odd writing just above the panels would explain all of it, if only he knew what they meant. He trailed his hands idly along the carvings as he moved forward, noticing elven faces as well as other faces, strange and foreign-looking to his eyes, and recurring themes of shooting stars, swords, and broken moons. At the end of this hall of images, the four warriors that had graced the outside chamber came into his sight. They flanked a door, plain and rather ordinary looking, save for another four-fingered and more stylized hand in its very center and a line of the strange runes to the right of it. There didn't seem to be a latch, handle, or visible lock, Bean realized after studying it closer

"A door with no key," he murmured to himself. He felt very stumped indeed.

He ran his hand along every inch of the doorway, pushed, prodded, and knocked everywhere along the wall. Nothing budged and nothing indicated any kind of entrance, except for this maddening hint of a door. Bean eventually settled down at the foot of the wall and sighed heavily. He put his chin in his hand and looked up at the four stone warriors gazing down on him. The fourth warrior's head had been vandalized, deliberately. Bean finally understood this from the indication of chisel marks around the shallow hole where the head should have been. Bean got back to his feet and gazed at the headless warrior.

"Tell me how I get through," he whispered fiercely. He looked over at the other figures. "Any of you. Just... mmf!... tell me already! What's the whole point of having a door if it can't be opened?" As he expected, none of the figures answered him. Bean folded his arms and slumped against the door, letting his chin drop mournfully to his chest. He stared at the floor and puzzled over his dilemma.

The silence wrapped itself around him, as the minutes or hours perhaps trickled by. Bean listened to the quiet so intently; until after a while, it almost seemed it could be a sound in itself, a mind-numbing drone as dark brown and thick as molasses. He could hear his heart beating in his chest, his steady breathing and before long, the annoying buzz that comes from listening too hard and too long to nothing rang in his ears. He rubbed his nose absently and sighed.

Then he raised an eyebrow.

"Huh?" he muttered to himself. "What... what is that?"

As he tilted his head, he glanced around in perplexity, becoming more aware that on the edge of his hearing, the silence had gently unfolded into music, a soft rhythmic strain that he couldn't distinguish as any tune he ever remembered hearing. It increased steadily, but Bean couldn't pin it down as either pure music or a chorale of voices. It seemed words floated into his head as he listened, but if they were words, they were in a language he had never heard before. He rubbed his face slowly and leaned closer to the door.

"Ohh," he breathed, as he closed his eyes in bliss. "It's the song..."

Intense emotions rolled in waves through his heart; pride, sorrow, joy and pain both fierce and exquisite far beyond any heroic ballad or a whistling farmer's tune. A hard lump formed in his throat as he gave a long shuddering sigh and finally opened his eyes again. He felt vaguely surprised to realize tears streamed freely down his face. He hadn't even realized he had been crying. Feeling a bit sheepish about that, even if no one had been around to see it, Bean hastily pulled his hand into his sleeve and wiped his face dry, as the song faded into the recesses of his mind and yet somehow didn't completely vanish.

Feeling drained and giddy from the odd incident, he placed his hand on the carving in the middle of the doorway to steady himself and straightened up in sudden shock, when the panel shifted beneath his touch with a loud scrape of stone.

"So that's the trick!" he exclaimed as a relieved grin broke across his face. He cracked his knuckles, bit his lip in grim determination, and shoved at the panel as hard as he could. It moved inward steadily, until it suddenly fell away with a loud echoing crash and a rising cloud of dust. Bean pulled himself up into the narrow hole and slid himself forward.

That same bluish light hit his face again with a vivid intensity that made him squint a little. He heard a murmuring noise, not anything made by human voice, but rather like wind whistling through drifts of snow, a cold dry mournful noise. Bean wriggled his way through the hole, waving away the drifting dust, and dropped down on the floor.

He lifted his head and his vision cleared as the dust began to settle. Then his heart started to thud a little faster as he heard the song again.

In the silent hallway behind him, the four stone warriors kept their vigil at the door as they had done for centuries. A breath of cold air stirred lightly across the floor and the crystals dimmed. For the briefest moment, the hard-carved edges of the fourth stone warrior softened and blurred. In the ruined face, eyes of white fire slowly burned into existence. They shifted their attention towards the door, narrowed to flickering slits... and then faded as quickly as they had appeared. The bluish glow of the crystals flowed back into life once again illuminating the ornately decorated hallway that otherwise seemed quite undisturbed and peaceful, right down to the carvings of the stone figures guarding the door.

Bean stood now in a vault with white walls of polished and closely fitted stone. Colonnades lined the walls with false doorways between, all surmounted by half-moon panels inlaid with fragments of mirrors and semi-precious stones. On either side of Bean stood alcoves from which gazed the stern visages of noble elvish lords, all crowned with

intricately fashioned headdresses of silver and gold. Their stone necks were hung with dried and moldering wreaths of fragile gray flowers, necklaces of green copper inlaid with tarnished silver, moonstones, and strange amulets of rotting leather and wood. Directly above his head, lines of inset silver and milky-white crystals created a dizzying and elaborate pattern of interwoven circles and lines. At the far end of the vault, a wall covered in carved runes depicted more mysteries, a shattering moon, two more stylized hands similar to the one that had been on the door, and a sword that bled. A few skeletons lay sprawled across the floor.

Bean might have taken closer note of all these things if he hadn't been so transfixed by what stood directly in front of the wall. The source of the brilliant light and the strange burbling murmur came from a simple round stone altar in the direct center of the room. Above it, a sword hovered motionless in the air within a wavering column of blue luminance that extended from the altar to a huge jagged crystal imbedded in the ceiling. Wreathed in eerily illuminated wisps of smoke or steam, its blade gleamed wintry-white. Bean stumbled forward until he stood directly at the altar. He climbed up on its edge and gazed up at this wondrous weapon as that haunting music twined around his mind. Nothing existed now except the song and the sword.

He reached up, standing on his toes.

His hand closed eagerly around the black leather-bound hilt.

The curling tendrils of smoke suddenly blasted outwards from the sword as a loud hiss filled the air. Blue light traced the pattern of veins all the way up his hand and arm. His eyes widened and shone a fierce intense blue suddenly, as in his mind the song burst all at once into a relentless surge of sensations and emotions. Memories of faces, stories, songs, and battles darted in quick succession behind his eyes like the moonlit flash of an owl's wing.

Bean wept again without self-consciousness or shame. He

wept for memories and sorrows he didn't even fully understand, for something far beyond himself that had been lost forever in the circles of eternity.

In another instant, he came back to his senses and found himself jumping down lightly from the altar with the sword clutched in his hand. His breath came in shudders and he shook his head and rubbed his face and eyes with the back of his shirtsleeve. He gazed around in a bewildered sort of way and then looked down at the sword he held. He gingerly ran his fingers along its scored edge as the clinging smoke drifted away. The blade was still sharp after who knew how many years and his thumb rubbed over the stone inset in the simple cross hilt, a dark-colored crystal with faint glittering threads of brilliant green that pulsated erratically deep within its heart. Yet despite the mystical qualities of the stone, it appeared plainly to be a sword made for battle, not some pretty ornament to hang from a belt. It had been used in the past. The blade, though well cared for, bore the numerous scars and scuffs of war.

If he hadn't been studying the sword so intently, Bean might have paid closer attention to the doorway from which he had come and the wall of runes and engravings that surrounded it. Even as he stood there, the carved runes melted and blurred together as the eyes of white fire smoldered silently into life behind him. The eyes narrowed and flickered with unreserved rage as they grew larger and larger.

Bean shivered and rubbed his arms. The temperature seemed to have dropped without warning. He glanced back in alarm as the floor, walls, and ceiling began trembling.

A second later, a deafening roar of fury robbed his senses as his world violently exploded into a shrapnel-punctured blast of shattered rock and mirrors that flung him backwards against the far wall.

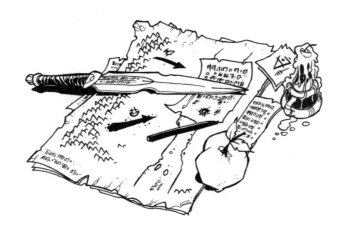

the Badger

Siv found himself in a partitioned-off section of the larger tent and carefully slid along the wall with his sword in his hand. A dim light from a flickering lantern attached to the ceiling let him better see his surroundings. In the corner stood a roughly constructed table of stretched hide, poles, and animal bones with a keg draped in more skins for the seat and a wooden bowl of fruit on the floor beside it. As far as decoration went, numerous spearheads and sword hilts, presumably trophies of vanquished foes, hung everywhere from the roof of the tent; a roof so low one would have to duck down in order to keep from running into them. Maps and scrolls tacked up on large screens made of animal hides and lashed-together tree limbs stood everywhere and several more official looking papers and scrolls sprawled across the table. Siv raised an intrigued eyebrow. He looked over at the tent-flap, taking note of the shadow of a guard's feet blocking out the crack of light along its bottom edge. He was careful not to send any of the dangling trophies swinging and clattering into each other and give himself away while he made his way toward the table.

He slid into the seat and studied the parchments laid out

before him, committing to memory significant numbers, troop formations, battle strategies, and other information. He noticed and recognized the emblems of many indigenous goblin-tribes; the Wolvm Claws, the Black Spears, the Red Teeth and Brothers of the Iron Blade. As he silently pushed aside a few papers, he came across a listing of battalions. Goblin tribes, he knew, were notorious for not getting along well with each other, yet according to what lay before him, someone had still managed to unite these quarrelsome tribes under the same military standards, a remarkable task to say the least. His fingers skimmed down the column of tribes serving under one insignia, noting the numbers. He turned over that page and paused.

Here on the next page was the name of the head officer of this particular regiment, one Laskin, goblin chieftain and prince of the Bronze Talons tribe. Above him ran a separate line of stark black elvish runes with an identification number and an unfamiliar rank symbol. From the general position of the symbol and the elvish writing, Siv guessed that the runes held the name of Laskin's commanding officer. Siv's lips moved silently as he translated the elven language. Then his mouth grew thin and hard. It was not a name as he thought, but only a word. Gren-el.

Siv glanced over at the map nearest to the table, tacked up on a hide screen. It crudely outlined Darkleaf and the Windy Mountains. The names of several settlements and towns were scrawled across the parchment in red ink and circled. Those closest to the Windy Mountains range had been crossed out and very near to the last town marked out, the names Heartleaf and Culvenbell on the edge of Darkleaf's sister forest, Cold Leaf, stood out in glaring red. Siv's eyes traced the path of conquest and suddenly, his eyes narrowed and grew hard. Above the names of several forts, a final name, written in larger red letters than the rest had been scrawled across the map.

White Stone Hall.

The sudden clatter and clink of trophies swinging against each other as someone came into the next room made Siv glance up quickly at the entryway. He heard a curse followed by voices in low conversation as well as the sound of people moving around and chains dragging across the earthen floor. Raising his sword and leaving the table, Siv edged over to the flap and peered through the cracks.

Beyond where he stood, Siv could see a larger room and caught the glint of loot in the corners and the gently swaying trophies hanging from the ceiling. A huge shadow loomed up in his vision and Siv moved back a little from the tent flap.

"...And why again does this concern me?" came a growl edged with impatience. "Isn't Gularh the commanding officer over the Iron Deep 31st regiment? Why did you not take this matter to him to begin with, goblin?"

An uncomfortable silence drew out through the air before the one being addressed finally answered, "Gularh be of the Ghost Arrows kindred."

The shadow blocking his line of vision moved again and Siv positioned himself once more at the tent flap. He found himself looking at two miserable-looking goblin soldiers, both badly wounded, bruised, and in shackles, being watched over by the guard he saw earlier. A tall savage-looking warrior passed by them and settled himself down on a folding stool flanked by two more human soldiers. He glared levelly at the two goblins as he folded his brawny arms.

"Tribe names are not an explanation for nine dead soldiers over the past three days,"

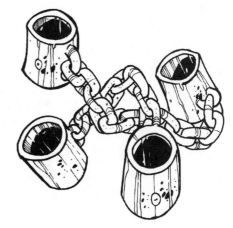

he grunted, lowering his eyebrows. "I want to hear more as long as I must sit in here wasting my precious time." The goblin's lips tightened and he said nothing else.

One of the soldiers leaned in towards the huge man and Siv noticed he wore the trappings of a higher rank officer. "Lord Badger, as tribal affairs are my area of understanding, might I now speak?" he asked. The Badger motioned for him to do so.

"Lord, if I understand correctly, the Ghost Arrows broke off from the Brothers of the Iron Blade about five generations ago and still offer a blood-levy to them. The Brothers are indirectly involved in this latest dispute between the Yellow Eyes and the Stone Staffs due to the eldest son of the ruling family being made a blood-son of the Yellow Eyes two years past," said the officer.

"Meaning?" said the Badger with an impatient snort.

"There are conflicts of loyalty under the old goblin weregild laws." The officer indicated the first goblin. "According to the law, he has every right to this Yellow Eye's life, since the Yellow Eye had earlier murdered kindred of his tribe. Simply put, the Ghost Arrows cannot get involved."

The Badger swore and glared at the first goblin. "So this is more of that accursed secretive right-of-blood business?" he demanded and the goblin said nothing, only bared his teeth at the one standing next to him and looked down at the ground. The Badger stood up again and approached the two goblin soldiers.

"Take off both their shackles," he instructed the guard. Siv raised an eyebrow as he watched the guard follow through with the instructions. Then, without warning, the Badger whipped out his knife and drove it into the gut of the Yellow Eye.

Siv heard the goblin wheeze in agony and saw him fold up over the knife. The

Badger gave the handle a vicious twist and callously shook the dying goblin off of the blade. He crumbled to the ground, his limbs rigid in torment. The smell of blood hung heavy in the air.

"Take him out of here. Hang him on the walls of the stockade as a warning," grunted the Badger. As the guard caught the goblin under his arms and dragged him away, the man turned his black eyes towards the other goblin. A broad hand caught the goblin forcefully by the throat and pulled him off of his feet as the Badger walked past. The huge man slammed the creature into the main tent pole so hard that Siv felt the whole place shudder.

"Listen well to me," the Badger snarled. "I care nothing of your tribal feuds or your blood-rights, but I will have order so long as I command this army. You, goblin, are a soldier in the Iron Deep 31st. Your precious azhlars are your commanding officers now and they serve under me. So long as I am here, you obey me."

He looked over at the two officers. "Let this fellow also hang by the dead one for three days without food or water. If he's still alive at the end of that time, cut off both his thumbs and let him wear them about his neck," he ordered. "Inform Gularh as well as the other commanding officers to tell these Yellow Eyes and Stone Staffs and Sagging Bellies and whatever other tribes that if these secret vendettas and claims to blood do not stop, I will start flaying alive a tribe member a day and personally feed their heads to the gren-els. Is that understood?" At their nods, he dropped the half-strangled goblin to the floor and waved at the soldiers to take him away.

"That is the only language goblins understand," he added over his shoulder with a grim smile. Siv slipped hastily back into the shadows as the burly man lumbered towards where he stood.

The Badger swept aside the tent flap and made his way over to the table. "Be-cursed little beasts and their dead quarrels... too many things to be done," he muttered under his breath, as he shuffled through the documents for a few minutes and the trophies swayed wildly around him. He rolled up a few papers, jammed them into his belt, and managed to knock over the bowl on the floor and scatter fruit everywhere, as he made his way back out again.

An apple rolled under the table towards the tent wall and a foot reached out and carefully stopped it in its path. Several minutes passed as the collection of hilts and spearheads settled down again and the mutters of the Badger faded off into further rooms. When all had fallen silent once again, Siv emerged from the shadows behind the screen where he had hidden himself. He eyed the tent flap for a moment and then sat back down at the table to quickly scan through the remaining documents.

Turning over a couple of them, he pulled out a nub of soft lead from a pocket in his coat and began jotting down necessary information on the backs of a few of the papers, as well as making crude copies of battalion formations and the maps. When he had written down as much as he could, he rolled the documents up and carefully hid them away on his person. He then glanced down and picked up the stray apple. A thin humorless smile stretched across his face as he tossed it up in the air, caught it, and then tucked it into his cloak.

He slipped back outside again in the pouring rain and traveled along the outside walls of a series of smaller annexes connected to the huge central tent by corridors of dripping tarpaulin and lashed together frameworks of wood. He stopped at the sound of feet squelching through the mud ahead of him and quietly made himself scarce behind a large pile of kindling and discarded armor.

Several goblin soldiers walked by, talking to each other in low voices:

"...Just found 'im by the alyta-pens not an hour ago. Yes.... body of a Hawk Blood with his neck broken so they say... there'll be trouble soon from the Sons of Fire over that, watch and see. They been waitin' for a chance to get back at their azhlar for three months now..."

As they vanished, Siv came out from his hiding place and glanced back over his shoulder, with a sudden thoughtful expression on his face and picked up his pace a little as he walked on. As he stepped over a couple of ropes tethered to the ground by stakes and rounded the corner, he found himself in a narrow semi-sheltered courtyard between the tents. He soon realized with sickening swiftness that had been the worst possible mistake he could have made.

In the pouring rain, not five strides ahead of Siv, the gren-el stopped in mid-lurch and raised its muzzled head. They regarded each other for a second that seemed to last ages. The creature's nostrils flared as it whiffed the air. The muzzle dropped to the muddy ground with a careless flick of a claw.

Water ran in thin trickles from strands of limp gray hair and collected in the corners of its sunken staring eyes. The thing grinned at Siv, as its breath hissed softly between gore-stained fangs. Then it hurtled straight towards him.

Thought ceased and Siv reacted with skills that so many years deep in exile could never dull. As the gren-el suddenly covered the last two strides in a powerful bound, Siv's hand snapped up and hurled the apple into the gren-el's vision. His cloak billowed outwards. He dodged, spun, and brought his sword around in an eye-blink of a moment, breathing his will and the force of the strike directly down to the very tip of the shining blade. The creature's predatory instincts could only focus on one thing in mid-leap and it fatally exposed its neck as it automatically snapped at the first thing that came at it, the apple.

An arc of black blood slapped across the canvas of the nearest tent.

The massive body of the gren-el slammed into the muddy ground, as Siv rolled and leaped to his feet. Its limbs twitched as it choked silently and with a faint wheeze, the creature fell still.

Siv collected himself for a moment and then raised his head and blinked back the rain running over his face. He felt a sudden coldness flooding out into his bones, a sure sign of the rapid approach of something else with the stink of a weave clinging to it. He sprinted quickly across the courtyard. The instant he saw the other gren-el, the creature had already burst out like a maddened dog from the shadows behind him to his right. Siv whirled and slashed desperately at the filthy grinning fangs and the gleaming eyes as his knee came around and drove into the side of its jaw, narrowly managing to deflect its path away from him and sending the gren-el skidding cat-like across the churned-up mud. As soon as he caught his balance, he dashed off. He couldn't afford a glance back or halt in his flight to finish the job. In only a matter of time, this commotion would be attracting attention and he had to get out of the camp and into the woods before that happened.

The gren-el scrambled back to its feet and turned, raising its head with some difficulty. A deep gaping wound ran from the corner of its nose all along the side of its face and blood dripped freely into the murky puddles across the ground. Its shoulders shook with silent mirth as it stood there panting. A long thin yellow tongue snaked out from between its teeth, licking away the fresh blood from its face with obvious relish. Then it took off once more after its quarry.

A couple of goblin soldiers caught a distant glimpse of the man when he burst from behind a tent with a sword in hand and his mud streaked hair fluttering behind him. Moments after he had vanished from their sight, a gren-el came bounding after him. It was more than enough evidence needed to quickly sound a general alarm. Booming drones of ram's horns and the frantic clacking of spears on shields began echoing into the dismal gray sky.

The front of Siv's coat hung in shreds and blood oozed from the marks of claws and teeth in his chest. Siv bit his lip against the pain. He barreled through a group of soldiers, taking out a couple in his way with a few quick and merciless strokes of his sword, and only just avoided the sudden wrath of the others as they drew sword and spear on him. Warding off the weapons, he broke free from the tangle of enemies, ducked into another alleyway, and kept on running. The shouts and curses of the soldiers behind him abruptly turned into screams as they caught the full fury of a blood-maddened gren-el who had no desire to see its pursuit interrupted.

In a matter of time, Siv had reached the alyta pens where he had first come in. As several soldiers ran out of various tents and alleys towards him, intending to hedge him in from both sides, Siv quickly scaled up the tall pen walls, swung over the top, and from there leaped lightly onto the broad backs of several alytas, hobbled and clustered

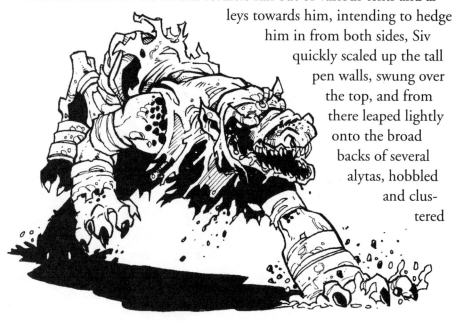

close together. The beasts grunted in sudden alarm and began shifting around, bumping against each other and the pen walls in the narrow space. Siv barely managed to keep his balance as he scrambled, half-walking half-crawling across their slippery rain soaked backs towards the opposite end of the pen. He jumped and caught the side of the pen wall and hoisted himself over it. Looking down he saw the cluster of thorn bushes and the sloping embankment leading down into the ditch now partly filled with water and mud from the pouring rain. He heard the rattle of the padlock being undone somewhere below him, and without another second's hesitation, he jumped.

He hit the embankment with a grunt of pain and slid down into the ditch. He sloshed rapidly across it, up the other side, and as he sped across the open space between the walls of the stockade and the safety of the forest, a delayed hail of arrows began bearing down on him. More than a few came too close to hitting him. Only luck and the misty curtain of the rain kept the aim of the archers inaccurate.

However, he knew he couldn't trust either luck or the weather to continue watching out for him. Even after he found himself once more beneath the leafy branches of the woods and the shouts and the noise of the alarms grew fainter behind him, he didn't dare pause to catch his breath. Instead, he doggedly continued at his same pace as the underbrush thickened and the ground began steadily sloping upwards again.

A single thought kept burning in Siv's mind as he drove himself onwards. He had to warn the Inn and Heartleaf and he had to warn them as soon as possible! Time and present circumstances, however, were definitely not working to his advantage.

The chase had begun.

Ganadon

Bean coughed miserably and opened his watering eyes to find himself staring at the base of a wall not two inches from his nose. Grit and the sour metallic taste of blood filled his mouth and a rough broken stone pressed painfully into the side of his face. Particles of dust lit by an eerie green glow drifted gently down towards him. He raised his head and stared dazedly, as an immense and shapeless shadow stretched itself up along the length of the wall and threateningly rose what looked like an arm. A low snarl echoed through the chamber. The noise of footsteps crunched quickly over the rubble towards the boy, then stopped again as the glow flooded brighter through the darkness. Bean heard breathing very close to him, curt hisses that sounded as though they came from between teeth clenched in tight fury. Slowly the arm lowered.

"Who are you, boy?" demanded a voice, as deep and harsh as the chiseled stone. It seemed as if the graven still figures of the elven lords had spoken from their alcoves. Bean rolled on his back with a groan, painfully propped himself up on his elbow, and sat up as the shadow retreated. The rope slid off of his bruised and bleeding side, its end frayed where the flying bits of rock had severed it in two. Bean rubbed his stinging eyes and spat on the floor. He realized his hand still clutched the hilt of the sword. It stood at an angle, the stone in its hilt gleaming a brilliant green, and the tip of the blade partly driven into the stone floor. Apparently, it had deflected a few good-sized pieces of wall in that position. He worked it free from the floor, wincing at the grating noise of steel on stone, and he wondered how in the world he had managed that.

"What do they call you?" came the deep voice again. Bean shakily got to his feet and rested his forehead against the cool pommel of the sword hilt to steady himself, as the green glow faded and the soft bluish light of the crystals filled the chamber once again. He could feel blood seeping into his hair and running down the side of his face from a cut on his temple.

"Bean... sir. M'called Bean," he muttered, not even knowing who he spoke to at the moment, but not really caring either. He hurt too much to think clearly. He blinked, rubbed his eyes again, and raised his head. His vision cleared, and all of a sudden, he gave a shout of terror and scrambled frantically backwards, falling over the rocks. The sword blade scraped and rang against the rocks, as his shoulders dug into the wall and his hand scrabbled around in fear.

A huge gray creature loomed over him, studying him with narrowed white eyes that smoldered and flickered like fire beneath a brow that jutted out like the overhang of a cliff. Indeed, the whole creature looked as though part of a cliff had decided to give itself a living shape somewhere between rock and humanity. A symbol stood out on its forehead, pulsing with the same fierce light as its eyes and a haphazard pattern of writing and symbols spread across its thick clay-like skin.

"Be still," it ordered in a calm voice and the boy obeyed without a word. "I'll not harm you. You call yourself Bean, little dustling?"

Bean wet his lips anxiously and replied, "Yessir."

The creature mused on this a moment. "'Tis a small name," it said finally with a thoughtful frown on its face. "And small be the hands that hold Ganadon's sword. Yet..." The brows lowered suddenly over the creature's eyes making it look even sterner.

"Your heart, boy. It must be read," it declared.

Bean's shoulders tensed and his face squinched up from sudden apprehension as the creature's massive hand reached towards him. The tips of two huge fingers rested lightly on the boy's chest with surprising tenderness and for a moment it just stood there in a deep and contemplative silence with its eyes closed. In the intense quiet, Bean felt his heart thudding in his chest beneath the creature's touch. The minutes trickled by. Bean allowed himself a soft sigh as he started to feel a bit awkward and fought the urge to squirm.

A tear dropped gently on the tip of his boot. The boy glanced up quickly at the creature. Wonder and a bit of puzzlement spread across his face, as he realized that this behemoth, which moments before had come roaring through a stone wall, had tears streaming down the side of its face. As it opened its eyes and withdrew its hand, Bean saw the smoldering fire fade and its eyes became as cool and luminously white as pearls. The blazing symbol flickered and slowly vanished from its forehead.

"That this sad world will yet yield a heart so pure," the creature murmured. "Such a gift... rare and precious in the darkness."

Bean wrinkled his forehead, unsure of the significance of these words. "What... who are you... sir?" he finally asked.

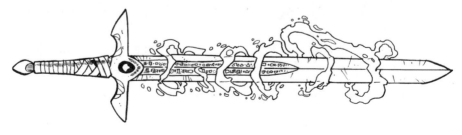

"Unimportant. A mere guardian and nothing more," came the reply. "And yet it seems my task is ended... now that you have come, little keeper of the sword."

Its eyes glanced down at a chunk of wall leaning on the floor. It ran its broad hand slowly across the writing.

"Pure of heart, of mind, of soul
The sword chooses whom it will hold.
Elven blood therein must be
For Ganadon's sword has chosen thee," said the Guardian.

"What do you mean?" asked Bean. He tried his best to take it all in at once, but it made his mind spin. "But... but it can't be. I'm no..." He looked down at the hand clutched around the hilt of the sword, recalling the stone hand in the hallway. For the first time in his life, the number of his fingers became significant, instead of just an oddity he had more or less accepted about himself.

"I'm no elf," he mumbled. He looked over at one of the mirrors that still stood and saw behind a veil of dust and a lacework of cracks, a bruised and battered little boy clutching a shining sword. He felt cold and peculiar inside because for a second, that little boy had become a stranger to him. He glanced down at the weapon in his hands again.

"You said Ganadon's sword?" he asked.

"Indeed it is, young one," the Guardian answered. "Somewhere within thee, elven blood must flow, for the sword did not consume your life and your mind at first touch as it did those others." The creature gestured to a shattered skull lying nearby. "It is thee who has become heir of Ganadon and none other can claim that right. Only you can restore what ought to be, even as those who rule now from the elven throne cannot."

Bean pondered this and heard a soft noise like hide being stretched over a frame. He raised his eyebrows as he looked up at the creature. Wisps of what looked like glittering steam had started drifting away from its massive body. Rimmed around its eyes and where the tears had run down its face, the skin had hardened into dove-gray marble, veined in delicate threads of silver. It slowly crept across the Guardian's face and over his forehead, even as Bean watched.

He couldn't help but ask. "What is that?"

The Guardian touched its face.

"My time fades as the star-shine," it said solemnly. "List, young guardian. Take heed of my tale and understand better thy heritage... and thy duties."

Bean nodded, tucked his legs gingerly under himself, and watched attentively as the Guardian eased back on its haunches and began to speak. Its solemn deep voice rolled through the empty chamber, echoing from the vaulted ceiling and walls.

"Far and ago, so say the singers of lore, the elven kingdoms slowly died amidst war and strife, bleeding out their light and life under the cold glitter of their foes' blades, the blades of goblin lords and their stone troll servants..."

Bean's eyes gradually closed of themselves, whether from extreme weariness or the strange lulling effects of both the voice and the song that had begun welling up again from the depths of his mind. Neither completely awake nor dreaming, he drifted through a strange sort of limbo and saw images behind the lids of his eyes, misty blurred images of suffering, battle, and smoldering cities all outlined in living silver and the song whispered to him in words both familiar and strange.

Bean opened his inner eyes and saw him, as clearly as if he stood in front of him. A young elven lord stepped out from the stone carvings and images of the dim chamber, stepped into life, and stood in the heart of a glittering blue fire. His dulled armor bore the scuffs, dents, and filth of battle instead of the dust and grime of the quiet centuries, his young face no longer a flawless carving but bearing numerous scars and wounds. Yet his eyes were cloaked in expressionless shadow. A tattered stained banner flew behind him with elven runes across it in frayed silver thread.

...Evernor held out for three days, so said the runners, but in the end they fell like the others...

...We cannot expect the help from Ovalstar and Havendale that we had hoped for in time...

...Dunsidne is the last... What are your words in this hour?...
...My lord?...

Bean heard the edge of fear in the calm voices of the dead. He saw Ganadon, the elven lord, lift his proud head to the sky and turn away in despair. The banner dropped and falling flakes of snow gently covered his family rune.

Yet in the rising darkness, rage burned, the rage of a soul unwilling to go gently into the unknown night.

Bean felt heat on his face, saw the glowing red of the forge, and heard the ringing of iron on steel. He smelled the smoke, the coppery odor of blood, and the grime and sweat of bodies exerting their strength upon anvil and ore.

"...Let them talk of dignified surrender. Let them accept the cruel whims of fate. We will not be forgotten names in a dusty scroll, not this day," Bean thought, realizing in the same instant that those thoughts were not his own. Gray eyes gleamed silver in triumph, as the song chanted words in Bean's mind, words that pierced and tore with the shriek of grinding steel on bone.

..Make it stronger... Make the blade stronger than any before it or any to come, came the whispers through the song. Call up the fire from within and drive it into the face of Time herself. Then shall you live forever, O elven king. Then they will always remember...

His hands reached out and grasped the spirit of the incandescent metal and pulled it towards him, shaping, twisting, and finally subduing it deep within the smoldering embers of his soul. The flames leaped up and became a sword shining through the swirling smoke, a sword with a pale white blade held at the level by a gauntleted hand. As it lowered, Bean saw Ganadon again, crowned and robed in sapphire flames that utterly consumed him.

"So the young elven lord, who had forged his soul within the metal of his blade went out to meet his enemies at the field of Dunsidne and determined to barter his life and the life of his people at the dearest of costs..."

The song grew pale and soft as Bean saw the dim sleepy light of dawn. The shadows of armed soldiers stretched across a white field. Branches and blades of grass stood motionless, glittering with frost. Banners snapped in the frigid breeze. Standing at attention before a faceless row of spears, swords, and dully-gleaming armor, Ganadon held his chin high. With a noiseless cry, he brought up his sword in an arc of glittering blue. The regiment swept like drifting snow down the embankment, as the shrill pipes became cries and screams, and the staccato roll of the flat-drums dissolved into the beat of blade on shield. Bean found himself whirled up in the chaos of battle. He forgot himself, as he fought with as much desperation and fury as the soldiers that surrounded him. Crimson blood stained the pure white snow.

As he fought, the din of war faded around him into a dim murmur like the distant hiss of ocean spray against the cliffs. The murmur of a thousand thoughts swirled around him. He stood at the eye of this storm, watching the goblins flee with spiteful screeches, watching the elves shout in hoarse victory, and allowed himself a slow sigh of relief.

Time abruptly blurred to a crawl.

He heard behind him the creak of a bowstring being drawn tight.

Bean turned and Ganadon turned.

The arrow released, slicing through the frigid air, cleaving the thick drifting smoke. Red agony burst behind his eyes and he fell gently forward into the snow.

In the curved reflection of a dimming gray eye, the sword spun through the air, hit the ground, and the shining white blade silently shattered into pieces. The frozen ground drank up his warm dark life. The frost crept gladly into his bones and splinters of ice blew across his face. Beyond the field of slaughter, a figure watched silently with dulled eyes that only a moment before had burned with envy and vengeance. A bow and arrows clattered across the dead blood-soaked ground, as the figure turned and walked off into the keening wind, his cloak trailing behind him like the wings of a raven.

"...Broken, crumpled on the plain lay the young elven lord in the snow... felled by a traitor's arrow, his sword shattered in two pieces," came the low quiet voice of the Guardian in front of him. Bean breathed in sharply and his eyes flickered open. His hand touched the back of his neck.

"I'm cold," he whispered. "So cold. It hurts."

He lifted his head up as his mind slowly cleared. He felt pain throbbing through the arm that gripped the sword, pain that had nothing to do with the cuts and bruises. He winced at the dissonant music wailing through his head and squeezed his eyes shut trying to silence it.

"She craves to be whole again, boy," said the Guardian and Bean opened his eyes. He saw the creature staring at the carvings running across the wall above both their heads with an indefinable expression on its face. A shadowed veil passed over the boy's eyes.

"I... I know your voice," he said, his tone strange and distant. "I knew your face. I saw it... Yes, I remembered it... Your name..."

The Guardian glanced down sharply at Bean. The boy blinked and his eyes clouded in confusion.

"No... No... I couldn't have! I'm sorry, sir. I..." He choked on his words and held his head in his hands as a painful wave of strong emotions surged over him. "I'm confused. I don't know what I'm saying," he murmured finally.

The Guardian studied the boy with a hard look on its face. "Heal her," it said to Bean. "You bring hope, young dustling. I cannot take back my error of pride, nor will I ever be the being I once was. It is too late for that. In you, however lies the chance of rebuking the tides of madness. This now is the task set before you and a truly formidable task it is indeed. Heal the sword and do not rest until it is done."

Bean lifted his head, heard the intensity of the words, and gazed at the sadness and the hope in the Guardian's white eyes. The glittering steam curled thickly around the creature now and patches of gray marble continued spreading across its shoulders, arms and legs.

Bean slowly got to his feet again. He looked over his shoulder at the intimidating pile of rubble blocking the door he had come through.

"But the Collector... The sword had called him. He said so," Bean answered faintly.

"Yet the sword has chosen thee, young guardian. She will answer to no other. The song has gone silent for thy companion."

"But... he'll kill me!" Bean exclaimed, his voice sounding shrill and thin as it echoed across the ceiling and walls.

The Guardian raised its brows slightly. "You are under a higher protection than you realize, Bean," it said solemnly. "Indeed, you are far more dangerous than you ever were. None can kill you now, be they warrior or weaver. Still, no weapon however powerful can shelter you from pain and suffering. You will know both intimately. So it shall be until you heal the blade of Ganadon."

Bean stood staring at his feet, lost in thought, and feeling very small indeed at this point. He sucked thoughtfully at a gap in his mouth where a tooth had been knocked loose. Then he looked up at the Guardian.

"But how do I heal a sword?" he asked. "I'm not a blacksmith. I don't know anything about forging steel. I wouldn't even know where to start."

The Guardian rubbed its chin thoughtfully. "The sword seeks out its own, young one, if you will trust where it may lead you. As to how to heal it... that I cannot say, I fear," it replied, and Bean sighed noisily and rubbed his forehead. "Yet there is an answer, Bean lad, and I trust you will find it, though I know not how. I do know you must prepare yourself for a rough and unsure path. That is part of thy duty...."

Bean only half-heard him. He had lifted up the sword and studied it as it lay in his hands. He turned it slightly and watched the dim light gleam across the edge and over the finely crafted handle. He admired the shine of the stone embedded in the hilt.

"I'm really holding the sword of Ganadon," he said softly to himself, and a touch of pride crept in his voice. "Wow..."

A sigh breathed warm on his hair. "Boy..." said the Guardian patiently. Bean glanced up and had the grace to look a bit sheepish.

"Sorry," he said hastily. "I understand. I think I do. But... how am I going to get out of here, sir, with the way blocked?" He glanced over at where the doorway had once been.

The Guardian moved stiffly to one side and gestured towards a gaping hole behind what remained of one wall. Bean dimly saw another chamber with the beginnings of roughly cut stairs leading up into darkness.

"Go... there," it said. "Follow... the stairs... You must hurry for your time dies quickly... and others will be hunting you... soon." The stone creature seemed to be having difficulty speaking.

Bean took a few steps forward and then turned back to the creature. "But where..." he began and then stopped as he saw that now both the creature's legs had become columns of solid marble rooted firmly to the floor. The full impact of the traitor's fate that had been sealed upon the Guardian finally hit Bean.

"What about you, sir?" he asked timidly. Something like a smile spread faintly across the creature's mouth.

"What... about me, Bean?" it answered. "I am... free... in a way..." It leaned down and picked up a bit of carving that had shaken

loose from somewhere, part of a young elven man's face. The creature stared sorrowfully at it, turning it around with rapidly stiffening fingers.

"My choices... brought me... to this end. Now... perhaps I... shall... know... peace..." it sighed.

"But..."

"Go..." The Guardian closed its eyes. "You... waste time..."

Bean held back. He felt an overwhelming wave of pity and sadness, watching the Guardian standing there, holding its bit of carving.

" ...Go..." came the deep voice again.

Bean stepped back a bit. Then he nodded, turned away, and started off towards the steps.

The Guardian listened to the patter of the boy's footsteps up the stairs echo and fade away into silence. Its head dropped down to its chest.

"That I... could... take back what... I had done," it murmured to itself. "My king... my friend... Ganadon. Find me... forgiveness... please..."

Its hands solidified into gray marble. The carving fell from its lifeless fingers and shattered across the floor as it opened its eyes and looked up.

"Or... is it... too... late..."

The marble crept across its mouth, covered its face and the Guardian fell silent forever. Its gleaming white eyes slowly ebbed away into lifeless hollow sockets in a face of expressionless stone. Its empty gaze remained fixed on the dark ceiling of the vault as its whispered plea faded into stillness. From somewhere farther away, a scream of rage echoed though the emptiness and darkness.

Betrayed

"Mmm?"

The Collector lifted his chin and turned his gaze to the opening at the foot of the facade as wisps of smoke danced away from his pipe into the darkness. He studied it a moment and then carefully snuffed out his pipe with his thumb, tapped the bowl on the floor, and tucked it away again, before he got a better hold on the rope stretched taut over the jagged lip of the hole and stood up.

He tilted his head. The corner of his ear twitched. Something, he sensed, had gone awry. He felt the song ebbing again, not in itself such an unusual thing. Many times before the song had slept, agonizing moments for the Collector, until its addictive and sweet melody surged back into life again. Still... those moments never lasted for long.

....Yet...

The Collector breathed in sharply and straightened himself up. His eyes widened. Seconds later, he felt a tremor run through the floor and up through him, the aftershock of a distant and violent concussion. The rope he clutched jerked this way and that and then abruptly fell limp in his hands.

He began rapidly hauling it in, hand over hand, the whole time knowing it came far too easily. As his apprehension mounted, a frenetic sort of energy seemed to take hold of him. He gave it one final savage jerk and the rope flew out of the hole and coiled at his feet.

The Collector stared down at the frayed end. The rest of the rope fell from his hand onto the floor.

Another failure, yes. Another gofer lost. That knowledge raked at his mind and with it came an even harsher realization that twisted the dagger in his back further. The song had fallen silent. It had abandoned him. He knew it as certainly as if his heart had stopped beating. Somewhere in his mind a door long sealed had flung itself open and a cold foul gale had come blasting through, freezing the blood within his veins, stripping down his very being to pale dead bones.

He clutched his ears as the breath came quicker and quicker between his clenched teeth. He heard the wind screaming in his mind. He threw back his head and screamed with it, screamed against the stillness of the centuries that settled mercilessly upon him and shattered him like glass, screamed until there was no breath left in him and the walls themselves trembled.

He staggered forward, holding his head, and one eye opened. His whole face twitched as he reached down and gathered up the rope and his sack. A strange hideous spasm of rage and grief twisted his mouth. He whirled around and flung everything in his hands to the far wall.

"Sing... sssingsingsing... alone... alone... all dead, all gone... traitors, traitorsss, betrayer... the boy betrayed us... Sing, I beg you, sing... It breaks, it falls, they fell... ice on the bones, the bones of the song, shattered... silence... alone... No... No... No... Lieeeeessssssss," he breathed out between his teeth.

He shook his head violently from side to side and clutched at his face. He slumped to the floor on his knees. As his mumbles gradually faded away, small shadows scattered noiselessly behind him through the antechamber. The dim light traveled in glints across the edge of numerous weapons.

Warily, they moved closer towards the cloaked still figure kneeling at the foot of the stone warriors.

The Collector's head hung down between his shoulders. His dulled yellow eyes stared at the floor. In the silence of the chamber, nothing could be heard but the sound of his own hard breathing. His eyes moved slowly to the corners of his vision.

"Do you think I cannot hear you?" he finally asked. His level voice sounded odd and tight as it echoed around the walls.

The Collector slowly got to his feet and lifted his head to stare up at the ceiling.

"Gone..." he whispered. "Gone." His hands trembled as they rose into the air, and he clenched them tight into fists. He spread his hands rigidly in front of his eyes as if trying to hide something from his sight, something he simply couldn't bear to see. His fingers curled.

"GONE!!!!"

The sudden screech of nails across stone made even the most hardened warrior among the goblins wince and clench his teeth. The Collector swept his hands away from the gouged stone with insuppressible violence and swung around. Blood stained the white stone and trickled from his hands. His cloak hovered in the air. His head hung low between his shoulders, but a wild and cold gleam in his half-closed eyes suggested he knew he was anything but a victim.

"Do you think... I cannot HEAR you?!?!" he called again. "I hear the beating of your hearts. I hear the breath between your teeth. I hear your very thoughts and the tainted blood moving through your veins!!!"

He spread his arms wide in an inviting gesture and chuckled. "I hear everything in this silence. Everything... save my song!!!"

His arms dropped by his side again, and he raised an accusing finger at the crouching darkness. His voice took on a more old-fashioned and aristocratic inflection as he lifted his head proudly.

"My song... and the voice of my people," he whispered. "'Twas not the bargain, Ric Noar. Ye fatherless bloody-eyed cur... ye scraper of slime and serpent's breath... ye treacherous whelp of the paling stars. Did ye not think I would realize in time?!? Grimwor and Midric have been devoured by the shadows. Mric Nettor has fled and Poraque is in chains, now ye are the last. SHOW THYSELF, RIC NOAR!!!!" A few of the goblins looked askance at one another, as the names of obscure ancestors hissed out between clenched fangs.

One warrior bolder than the rest separated himself from the menacing cluster of shadows, making silent gestures with his hands to his fellows to be silent a moment. His eyes narrowed in cunning. Curiosity at this mad creature's actions and perhaps a bit of mean-spirited intrigue had momentarily overridden his practical instincts of kill and be done with it all.

"Why be you here, troll?" asked the goblin softly.

"For the prize, Ric Noar... the prize I seek," said the Collector in a flat voice. "Cannot the wretched Azhlar of the goblin kindred go and leave us in our anguish?"

"We come for prizes as well... troll."

"And was not the blood of my people enough for thy appetite, Ric Noar?" hissed the Collector with sudden malice. "What then were those promises, I ask, those oaths sworn... that the Scroll of Ordinances was to be mine, that the Ring of the Judges would heed my voice and no other, that the earthdwellers would serve me? Lies, filthy lies the lot... you killed them all..."

"What prize seek you, then?" the goblin continued, keeping his voice deceptively gentle.

"Aye, killed them all, ye did!" ranted the Collector, ignoring the goblin and growing more agitated with every second. He jabbed a finger in the direction of the tunnel entrance. "Gaze upon what now lays at my feet... a kingdom of vermin and gnawed bones, its glory dimmed, its treasures despoiled and scattered! There is the worth of a goblin prince's words!"

"Yes, clever troll," said the goblin with a smirk. "But you tell us now what brings you here below.... to an elven shrine, yes? What hides here?"

"What is here is mine, Ric Noar," whispered the Collector, as his eyes grew hard. "It called me, claimed me, oh yes. It promised me power... power to raise this city from the ashes, to bring back the voices of my people, to make the halls shine again with the knowledge and songs of old..." The red rock troll appeared to be struggling with himself.

"Promises you know nothing of, goblin," he spat with sudden fervor. "What know ye of pride? What know ye of glory? Of redemption? Aye, the sword offered me all that and more... It..."

The Collector's expression abruptly darkened with doubt as his words trailed off. "Wait," he muttered, as he peered at the goblin standing in the slanted shadows. "Why does the mighty Azhlar of the goblins show such interest in my prize?" He lifted his head and breathed in the stale air slowly and realization spread across his face.

"Name yourself, goblin," he snarled deep in his throat. "Ye have not the reek of Ric Noar about you. Why do you stand thus and torment me with questions? Where is your prince?"

The goblin's eyes slitted in the darkness and his teeth gleamed in a taunting grin. "Pity the troll, lost in snow," he mocked. "Some things be better left untold, yes?"

The Collector grew still as a hunting cat. His hand reached down into one of his vest- pockets. "Very well," he said softly. "Games you like to play... I will bring ye out of the shadows then and show who is the master riddler here."

He brought his hand level to his eyes and spread his fingers. Between three of them, a suspension of multi- colored liquids trembled within gleaming glass-spheres. He flicked them lazily up and through the air. The spheres burst upon the stone floor with a curl of acrid black smoke and a dull "foomph!" that at once grew into a terrible and continuous roar as flames shot across the stone floor into all the darkened corners. The silent chamber suddenly resounded with screeches of surprise and pain and the shadows of scattering goblins danced crazily across the walls, illuminated by the sudden glaring glow of the fire.

From beneath a canopy of flames, the Collector emerged and stood with a detached and calm expression on his face.

"Ahhh... there ye are," he said, as the hue of the flames flickered from gold to ice blue. He started forward and the fire fanned across the floor in front of him, spreading and leaping higher with every step.

One of the goblins held

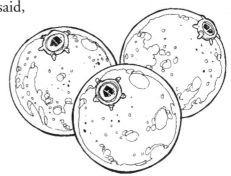

181

at bay by the unnatural fire gathered up a facade of courage born of desperation and sent a short spear hurtling at the maddened weaver. It caught the Collector in the shoulder and he staggered back for a second and gritted his teeth in noiseless pain as red soaked down the front of his clothing. Other goblins heartened by the fact that the creature could bleed, rushed at him through the flames, screeching battle cries. Just as they were upon him, the Collector reached up and wrenched the spear out of himself, gripped the blood-stained weapon in his hand as fire darted up the length of the shaft, and brought it around in a burning white arc. A couple of goblins fell beneath the edge of the spear, the rest darted backwards clawing and beating at each other and shrieking as the fire ate into the leather of their clothes, the wooden grips of their weapons, and made metal glow red hot. The Collector then whipped the fiery spear around his head. As the remaining goblins bore down on the weaver in a final rush attack, the flames ebbed towards him, retreating rapidly from the walls and floor of the chamber to whirl up around him in a blazing orb. As the orb slowly contracted around him and turned white, smoldering red cracks shot across the floor, the air shimmering with heat so intense the goblins at the front halted in mid-rush and fell back, holding up their arms and averting their eyes in terror.

The flames licked at the edges of the Collector's cloak. Fire encircled his face, reflecting in his dangerously gleaming eyes, and he felt nothing. He tucked the spear smoothly underneath his arm as his other hand came up. He snapped his fingers.

The entire chamber dissolved in a silent blazing fusillade of shining white.

Evening Errands

Thunder pealed across the sky as flickers of lightning made eerie wraiths of twisting branches hang heavy with tatters of gray-beard moss. Rain pelted the surface of a stretch of murky water surrounding the bloated trunks and dark knees of bone-white cypresses.

Beneath a half-fallen tree, a sloshing noise accompanied the whine and creak of badly rusted hinges as a long-disused trapdoor swung open. Water spilled over Bean's aching feet, as he pulled himself up out of the opening. He gazed out at the vastness of the swamp and sighed deeply as discouragement pelted down on him like the rain. After hours of walking in near darkness up an endless stone stairwell, it had been such a relief to finally think he had come to the end of his troubles. Now it looked as though he had only just begun the toughest leg of his journey. Nevertheless, he lifted up his sword, crawled out from beneath the log, and sloshed doggedly into the black waters.

Sometime later, twilight faded into night and the rain grew even more merciless. Beneath the dripping branches, Bean's head slumped between his shoulders and Ganadon's sword dragged in the water beside him. He wearily kept wiping away the rain from his face and his lower lip trembled from the chill in the air. He looked up, straining to see through the darkness and rain as terrible thoughts kept crossing his mind that he was simply going around in circles and he'd never see the end of this swamp. Mud and algae caked his boots and legs, making walking more and more difficult with every step. Bean's shoulders slumped lower.

He stumbled and plunged knee-deep in an unseen hole and fell down on his hands. He stayed like that for a long while, staring down at the black waters, not really seeing anything, and the rain pattered down on his head and ran down the sides of his face. His eyes fluttered. So easy to become as stagnant as the water he knelt in, to just stay there, to sink down into the darkness and give up completely. His head drooped lower and lower until his bangs trailed in the water and the breath from his nose and mouth hissed and seethed across the shimmering surface of the dead pool.

Then he abruptly muttered, "N-no. No..." to himself. His eyes flickered open again and glimmered faintly blue as the song of the sword urged life back into his faltering spirit. He jerked his head back up, crawled forward, and struggled back to his feet again. He stood for a minute, swaying slightly, then with a deep breath continued onwards. Every swamp had to end somewhere. He had to make himself believe that. He had to trust that only a few steps further into the night would bring him through to the morning.

Only a few more steps... that was all.

Lightning fluttered silently through the sky again. It briefly outlined something slipping almost noiselessly over twining roots, something eagerly following the scent of wounded prey through the dark waters, a scaled and monstrous horror that should have remained hidden in the night.

As Bean slogged onwards, his mind wandered over the words of the Guardian. He stopped in his tracks, lifted up the sword with some effort, and studied the blade as rainwater dripped from its edge. "Heal her," echoed the words in the back of his mind and he saw again the mournful face staring down at the fragment of stone in its hands. "Yet what was there to heal?"

As if in answer to his silent question, cracks glowing faintly blue outlined themselves over the white blade and faded once more. Bean lowered an eyebrow in astonishment. He peered closer at the blade and rubbed his fingers thoughtfully across it. He felt the odd coldness of the blade creep into his bones and travel down his spine. He glanced up at his surroundings. Old childish fears of the dark and the unknown pressed down on him and dim unpleasant memories surfaced of being pulled along by the wrist through night-shadowed woods with some unseen and frightening foe always only a step or two behind.

"Quick now, boy, stir those liddle stubs of yours," his voice whispered in Bean's ear. "If they catch us, it's all over... You and your ol' da'll be gallows-fruit, for certain... Faster, now..."

He looked over his shoulder and tilted his head. Over the roar of the rain, he thought he had heard something, the snapping of a branch somewhere. He swung the blade onto his shoulder as he tried to shrug off his fears. Even so, his pace quickened a bit as he moved on.

Only minutes later at the very place Bean had stood, eyes emerged quietly from the water and blinked slightly as droplets of rain struck them. The slanted pupils widened, adjusting themselves to the darkness before a thin clear film slid back over them once more and the thing vanished smoothly beneath the surface of the water in a trail of black bubbles.

Bean staggered on until finally he couldn't push himself to take another step. His legs felt like lead and throbbed painfully. Bean sank again into the muck beneath a dark cypress. Shivering, he leaned against the trunk, drew up his legs, and folded his arms across his knees. He laid his forehead on his arms and silently promised himself to rest for only a little bit. He coughed feebly, sneezed, and cleared his burning throat with a wince. His stomach grumbled, irritated at being neglected for so long. He rubbed it unhappily and tried to hold his eyes open.

Somewhere close behind him, water sloshed gently. Bean raised his head, as a deep and unreasonable terror surged once more overcoming his hunger and weariness.

"Stop it," he whispered severely to himself. "It's nothing... a fish... a falling branch..." He slid over to the other side of the trunk and peered around through the rain and the blackness. Nothing, but the dim white outlines of trunks and blurred shadows met his gaze. He heard nothing but the splashing of the rain, yet he still felt the skin prickle across the back of his neck.

He started sliding back, turned his head, and then froze.

Warm fetid breath brushed through his hair as a low growl rattled only inches away from his face. Lightning brightened the sky and outlined in hideously clear detail the curve of fangs beneath a blunt snout and the predatory shine of small black eyes. In the pitchy blackness, Bean's eyes whitened in horror.

The creature lunged.

Bean reacted without thought. If a hand had come out of nowhere and snatched him away, he couldn't have possibly moved faster. As if in a dream, he felt himself vault easily up over the creature's shoulder, sword in hand, as the beast's thick skull smashed into the trunk of the tree and its claws and teeth gouged chunks out of the wood. The blade shone a brilliant blue and fine cracks shot across its steel like veins of fire. That same brilliant light flickered in the boy's blue eyes, illuminating them with a determined ferocity, not even the boy understood.

He splashed down into the water, leaped up, and ran. Seconds later, the creature came smashing through the trees after him and rammed into him from behind, knocking him completely off his feet into the murky depths of a pool.

Filthy black water filled his eyes, ears, and mouth as he spi-

raled weightlessly down and touched the spongy bottom. By the eerie blue glow of the sword, he saw the shadow of the enormous creature twine itself gracefully through the water and hurtle straight at him. Bean spun backwards through the water and a silent scream of agony escaped his mouth in a stream of bubbles as those jaws gaped ravenously, clamped down on his lower leg, and jerked him viciously upwards.

Some sort of restraint broke inside the boy. Instead of the paralysis of fear and pain, instincts not his own propelled his sword arm to curve around impossibly fast against the dragging weight of the water rushing around him. Just as the creature surfaced the pool, the blade slashed across its eye. It bellowed, as it flung Bean up into the air and he just narrowly missed having part of his leg torn completely away. As he twisted around in mid-air and fell, his focus suddenly became as sharp as a knife's edge. He heard the battle cry of his enemy and the smell of fire and blood filled his nostrils. The blade flashed in front of him as he plummeted downwards and he thrust it with vicious force straight between the fangs of the creature, as the jaws closed on his arms and the murky water swallowed them both up with a tremendous splash.

The waters churned and thrashed about violently for a few minutes. Then they gradually grew still. A deep uneasy silence descended upon what had only a short while ago been a scene of desperate chaos.

With a splash and a painful gasp, Bean suddenly broke through the surface of the pond clutching the hilt of his sword in his hand. The glimmering blue blade of his sword was stained black in triumph.

Coughing violently, he swam until his feet touched bottom again. He dragged himself up an embankment, crawling painfully on his hands and knees through ankle-deep water. From his elbow down, his sleeves had been ripped to shreds, soaked in the black blood of the creature, mixed with his own blood. Lacerations crossed his chest and his leg throbbed with incredible pain, and he shivered uncontrollably.

He made it as far as the foot of an old rotted-out water oak. With his last remaining bit of strength, he dragged himself inside the belly of the old tree, turned over on his side and finally allowed himself to collapse in the cold watery muck. The hilt of the sword slid from his loosened fingers and the blue glow of its blade faded. Bean slowly curled up in a tight ball of misery.

He thought he heard someone singing off in the distance as he fell gently into a blissful oblivion.

***

"Little one, be silent a moment, please... Papa is listening..."

The merry little song fell silent as the man held his lantern up. He turned his head and stared off into the darkness, the rain pattering down around him. He shifted the weight of the axe on his broad shoulder a bit as his face turned thoughtful. Finally, he started walking off toward the edge of the swamp.

Around his head a tiny delicate fae-creature, seemingly fashioned of starlight and sunbeams fluttered inquisitively between the raindrops.

"How long is a moment, Papa Theron?" came a little voice like the chiming of a silver bell. "Is it as long as 'just a bit' or is it more like 'in a while'?"

Theron, the tall burly man with the axe smiled as he walked. "That's a good question, my little Tia-pho-phia. Perhaps it's somewhere in between."

"Well... then my is thinking we've been gone for longer than a moment. Mama will worry about Papa, yup," answered the pretty little pixy.

"Just as soon as I see what all that commotion was about a moment ago, little one."

"Ohh, be careful, Papa... Mama will be none too happy if you get hurt!"

"My Tia-pho-phia, you needn't worry about me... I've been through too many close shaves before and I shan't be making Mama upset tonight either," replied Theron gently, as he sloshed through the watery sludge.

"She warned me to be keeping a careful eye on you. My am keeping both of them... See?" The pixy made a show of opening her eyes wide with her tiny fingers. Her eyes were a bright and solid apple-green without pupil, irises, or whites.

"I see..."

"Nooo, Papa... My sees you, yup." The pixy giggled at her own clever little joke. "Yup... good watch-fae my am. Do jobs good... Keep papas out of trouble, my do."

"Really..."

"Yup, really."

Tia flittered down and sat down on the edge of the lantern beneath the tin shade with her back to the warm glass. She daintily stretched out her little hummingbird-like wings and buzzed them vigorously to dry them off. The iridescent feathers shone and glimmered like opals as the lantern-light hit them. Her tiny feet kicked busily as she talked.

"Lots of raining this season, no? My thinks there is more than last season. Mama must be happy about that, yup. She likes the rain..."

"I would think so..."

"Yup, my thinks so too, yup. Though my don't like nasty rain at times," Tia made a face as she folded one of her wings around herself to preen for a moment. "Spoils my wings. You think my wings are beautiful, don't you?"

"I think all my little pixies are beautiful, wings and all."

"But my am the prettiest, yes?" asked Tia.

"Now, my Tia-pho-phia, why are you trying to get me in trouble?"

"Ohh, my wouldn't do that. Tia looves Papa Theron, yup," the pixie said earnestly. "Big important papa you are, make Mama happy. Been many a moon before you came that Mama cried for someone special and oh how Mama loves you, yup!"

Theron had to smile at that remark. "And I do love Mama, yup. She keeps me sane."

Tia giggled again, a merry little sound in the darkness and rain. "You yupped like Tia!" she exclaimed in delight.

"Yup."

"Yup. Yupyupyupyup..." the pixie chanted and then stopped when Theron paused in his tracks and glanced around.

"This seems like the right direction it should have been coming from," he mused, as he lowered his lantern and scanned the ground for any telltale signs. "Hm...That might be a track there."

"Ohh, let me see, let me see... Good tracker my am, yup."

"I don't doubt it, Tia-pho-phia. Here you are..."

Theron held the lantern lower for her as Tia cocked her

head and studied the print of a small foot in a patch of soggy ground.

"It's still very fresh. See the rain hasn't completely washed it away yet," Theron explained.

"Tiny, tiny print... not tiny as Tia though. It's an earthdweller?" she asked.

"I'm not sure," said Theron thoughtfully, as he raised his lantern up. "Ah, see Tia... There's where someone's muddy hand brushed against the tree-trunk." He took another couple of steps forward and showed her the print across the hairy bark, a print badly smeared, but still discernable as a hand.

"One, two, three, four. Four fingers like Tia," said the pixie. "My thinks it is a earthdweller."

"Tall for an earthdweller, yet still short for a human."

"Ohhh... a very big pixie then!" Tia's eyes widened in wonder at the thought of a gigantic pixie.

Theron chuckled. "Or elven, perhaps. Hmm... the mystery deepens."

"Hmm," echoed Tia, as they moved on.

Not long after that, they discovered the ruined tree, its trunk nearly in splinters from the effects of teeth and claws. "He got angry at the tree," Tia concluded and looked very sad. "Poor tree..."

Theron lifted his axe off of his shoulder and his face grew more serious and alert. He could smell the faint musk of a blunt-nosed gharaym in the air. "My little Tia, come here and climb inside the herb-bag," he said, as he opened up his coat. The pixie darted through the air and landed on one of several large leather satchels hanging from his belt. She pulled open the lid and snuggled down inside a large bundle of fragrant white-stemmed herbs topped with lacy blue flowers.

"Papa is not scared, is he?" she asked as she pulled the lid back down over herself.

"No, because he has his Tia close by. Now, no more talking,

please," he said firmly.

A few more strides brought him to the edge of the pool. He glanced around with his axe held at the ready. Here the musky odor was very strong, but the smell of blood was even stronger. Theron frowned and circled the pool, careful not to get any closer to it than he could help. A gharaym that had just eaten its fill nor- mally didn't pose a threat but best not to take chances.

A thin pitiful moan made him turn his head quickly. He lifted the lantern and saw deep in the shadow of a rotten water oak, something lay curled. Theron came closer, knelt down, and the golden glow of the lantern fell upon the bruised and muddied pale face of a young boy.

"By the broken moon," Theron breathed, as he sat his lantern and axe off to one side and reached inside the oak.

"What is it?" came the muffled little voice of the pixie. The satchel-lid flipped open and Tia peered out curiously, as Theron pulled the boy out and cradled him on his knee.

"Oh... what is that? Another papa like you?"

"No, my Tia. He's a human like me, but he's only a little lad. Here let's get a better look at you, son," Theron murmured. He picked his lantern up again and held it over the boy. An appalled expression came over his face as he saw the extent of the injuries.

"Oh! The liddle laddie's hurt... oh no good, no good..." squeaked the pixie.

Theron patted the side of the child's face and laid a broad

gentle hand on his forehead. He felt the boy stir feebly in his arms and moan again. "Easy, lad," he whispered. "Oh, Tia, he burns with fever. Head back to Mama as fast as your little wings can take you. Tell her I come and tell her what I have. Hurry now... this child could die."

"Yes, Papa, my go." Tia darted out from his coat and flew off into the night.

Theron picked up his axe and slid the butt of it through the ring at the top of the lantern. He stood up and held the lantern in front of him as he strode off the way he had come, with the boy lying limply in the curve of his arm.

"Hold on there, boy," he said, as he looked down anxiously at the little fellow. "We'll get you help. I've gathered night-blooming bindwort all this evening and I daresay my sweet wife can find good use for it now. Hold on there. Poor little lad... he's so cold..."

The edge of his thumb brushed tenderly through the boy's matted hair as his expression darkened a bit. The boy's lips, dark blue from the chill moved noiselessly and suddenly his eyes flew open and widened as they slid from side to side, seeing nothing but his own fever-dreams.

"Ganadon... did cry... the endless night.... a blade, broken... in sorrow... fright... die... oh..." The boy breathed in sharply and tears of terror and grief ran slowly down the side of his fevered cheeks. "Die..." he sobbed pitifully. "Oh… he died... died..."

Theron felt his heart contract and pain creased his face. " No, lad, no. No one dies in Theron's arms. No one," he said softly, as he wiped away the tears. Whether it was to reassure himself or reassure the boy who lay in his arms, it was hard to say. "Go to sleep, little one. You're safe," he told the boy. He laid his hand gently on the boy's scruffy blonde hair, rubbing his thumb over the small forehead with its many cuts and bruises. The child stopped struggling and slid into restless slumber. Theron walked off and wondered silently to himself what a little boy was doing out here in the swamp in the middle of nowhere.

Behind him, abandoned and unnoticed as it lay in the deep murky darkness by the hollow tree, the sword glimmered faintly blue. A froth of black bubbles seethed quietly across the waters as the sword sank slowly out of sight into the muck. The blue glow faded into utter darkness and stillness filled the air.

to be continued...

Glossary

- **Azhlar** –*(Az-lar)* A Goblin chieftain in charge of a full tribe of goblins.
- **Badger (the)** – One of the chief most commanding officers in the assembled goblin army, a large human of considerable power, cruel and ruthless, responsible for enforcing order among the warring goblin tribes.
- **Bean** – Property of Gort the Ogre, boy servant in the Silver Dagger Inn. It is unlikely "Bean" is his real name, but it is the only name he has known. He is twelve years old, a hard worker, and despite Gort's insistence that no good thing will come of him, dreams of being reunited with his estranged father.
- **Beast King (the)** – The goblin's name for the one who united their warring tribes and drove them into the civilized lands "to hunt." Supreme commander of the goblin armies, the one who utilized the Gren-els that accompanied the goblin raiding parties.
- **Bindwort** *(Night-blooming)* – a swamp herb, blooms at night, used in an assortment of medicinal potions.
- **Black Spears** – A goblin tribe.
- **Blackclaw Pox** – A particularly nasty disease that is highly contagious, causes severe itching, and the fingernails turn black and fall out, giving the sufferer no natural ability to scratch oneself for relief.
- **Bloody Eye Flux** – An oft-fatal disease, which often leaves "lucky" survivors with severely impaired vision.
- **Bronze Talons** – A goblin tribe
- **Brothers of the Iron Blade** – A goblin tribe
- **Catmint** – An herb used for making a calming tea.

- **Chokecherry** – A bitter forest berry, popular with sloths.
- **Collector (the)** –A driven Red Rock Troll who is obsessed with collecting objects and artifacts of various worth and beauty.
- **Crimson Per** – An earthdweller merchant who travels the roads of Darkleaf, selling his wares. He is a family man, and has several children including Tannis and Fencer.
- **Crow-Eyes** – A regiment of goblin spies for the Beast King's army. They represent the elite of the goblin tribes, and are fiercely loyal to the Beast King. They serve as a form of secret police among the more unruly tribes when not engaged in spying missions abroad.
- **Cuffy** – a common name for a juvenile forest sloth.
- **Culvenbell** – An outpost and settlement near the Windy Mountains.
- **Dargle Shrooms** – An edible mushroom, used in ogre stew to disguise unsavory scents and flavors, such as rats and other unmentionable items that might find their way into Groggle's stews.
- **Darkleaf Forest** – The vast forested land wherein the Silver Dagger Inn was built. The townships and settlements in and around the forest are loyal to the White Stone Hall. They are under the authority of the young King David, yet are very independent and used to being ruled by their own internal councils. Darkleaf has been the site of many battles over time. The Ogre chieftain Morloss once claimed all of Darkleaf as his own. The forest at one time hosted multiple underground cities of vast wealth and power created by earthdwellers and red rock trolls. The two capitals were known as Tin Par and Felindah.
- **Darrow (Lord)** – A velumni house in White Bird Cove. Lord Darrow is young and impetuous and once the friend of Fencer Per, his chief security guard.
- **Dunsidne** *(Dun-sidney)* – An Elven outpost where Ganadon fought a great battle just prior to his forging of the blade.
- **Earthdweller** – Name for the Dwarven race that lived in the Land of the Broken Moon who built the vast underground cities with the Red Rock Trolls. These cities now lie empty and in ruin.
- **Earthdweller Brandy** – A strong alcoholic drink made by earthdwellers. Like most things of earthdweller origin, it is not

common knowledge how this drink is made, but it is one of the more costly drinks available in fine taverns.

- **Eldenberry (Wine)** – A sweet forestberry used in making wine.

- **Evernor** – A fallen Elven city, besieged by goblins and stone trolls. It fell in the time of Ganadon, after holding out for three days.

- **Fae-creature** – Tiny Spirits and Sprites that were blamed for any bad or good luck in the natural world. These generally friendly creatures are the embodiment of innocence, mirth, and whimsy, and are vastly intelligent, contrary to popular belief. They are not usually seen by humans, elves or other creatures of Dark Leaf.

- **Felindah** – *(Fe-lin-da)* One of several underground cities that lie in ruin beneath Darkleaf forest once belonging to a proud gathering of red rock trolls. It was the foremost underground city and the seat for the Ring of the Judges.

- **Fencer Per** –*(Fen-sir Pear)* the half breed son of Crimson Per, an earthdweller, and his human wife. Fencer has spent a great deal of time with Lord Darrow, a Velumni Lord in the Southern Human Kingdom of White Bird. Due to an unspecified incident he returned home to be with his family.

- **Forestwalker** – A name given to an individual who, through extreme training and discipline, becomes one with the forest. Usually associated to beings with mystical or magical power.

- **Fortune-bones** – A superstitious tradition of casting small animal bones, and attempting to interpret the patterns of how they fall for fortune telling.

- **Ganadon** –*(Ga-na-don)* An ancient Elven King who wove his soul into a sword, defended his people against impossible odds, slew many goblins, and then was betrayed by one of his own friends.

- **Gharaym** *(Ga-har-um) (blunt-nosed)* – A carnivorous, dangrous, reptilian swamp creature.

- **Ghost Arrows** – A goblin tribe.

- **Goblin Tribes** – Wolvm Claws, Black Spears, Red Teeth, Brothers of the Iron Blade, Bronze Talons, Ghost Arrows, Yellow Eyes, Stone Staffs, Sagging Bellies, Sons of Fire, Hawk Blood and Iron Deep 31st.

- **Goldenberry** – A sweet yellow forest berry, that often ferments on the vine, and can be easily brewed to make a liqueur.

- **Gort** – The ill-tempered Ogre owner of the Silver Dagger Inn, brother of Groggle.
- **Grand River (the)** – A massive waterway that proceeds from the ice floes of the far north, above the White Stone Hall, all the way down to the sea. It empties into the ocean at the south border of the Southern Human Kingdom. The Grand River forms the eastern border of Darkleaf Forest and is a major concourse for trade and traffic between the White Stone Hall and other realms.
- **Gren-el** – A creature that was once an Elf, who through the madness of the Weave, sought to use the weave's power on his own body "to perfect" it. Gren-els are cruel, greedy, power-hungry, and highly intelligent, believing they have perfected their physical form for the task of murder.
- **Grimnorp** –*(Grim-norp)* A goblin outpost with high stone walls, decorated with the bodies of dissident goblins and other unfortunate "dead" creatures.
- **Grimwor** – *(Grim-wor)* A name referenced by the Collector of someone in his past.
- **Groggle** –*(Grog-gle)* Brother of Gort, brewmaster, cook, and butcher. He takes care of the Bean.
- **Guardian (the)** – The Guardian of Ganadon's blade.
- **Gularh** – *(Gu-lar)* The Goblin commanding officer over the Iron Deep 31st regiment.
- **Hawk Blood** – A goblin tribe.
- **Heartleaf** – A town in or near Darkleaf Forest.
- **Hollow-stem Blight** – A plant disease that often infects whole fields of Honeyshrub.
- **Honeyshrub** – A cultivated bush named for its sweet leaves, used to make leafbrew.
- **Hopfly** – An annoying leaping insect that often ruins picnics in Darkleaf.
- **Iron Deep 31st** – A goblin tribe.
- **King David** – The young human king of White Stone Hall.
- **Kithdeer** – A skittish forest herbivore, that travels in herds throughout the woods. They are small, quick, and difficult to capture, blending into the forest underbrush easily.
- **Laskin** – The name of a Gren-el placed in command of a given goblin tribe by the Badger to rule over its azhlars.
- **Leafbrew** – A popular beverage at the Silverdagger. One of the house specialties, and one of Groggle's guarded secrets. It is

unlikely that leaves are the chief ingredient of the beverage.
- **Long Creek** – A town near or around Darkleaf.
- **Mab** – Crimson Per's multox.
- **Mama Fairy** – The caretaker of the fae-creatures.
- **Marathur** –*(Mar-a-thar)* An earthdweller homesteader living near the town of Pale Leaf, near the Silver Dagger Inn, the husband of Mayve.
- **Mayve** – Opinionated and irrepressible Earthdweller wife of Marathur.
- **Me-Lonar** –*(May-lo-nar)* The name of the Collector's underground abode.
- **Midric** –*(Me-dric)* A name referenced by the Collector, somehow related to Grimwor, who was connected to the Collector's past.
- **Moon-signs** – The fragments of the broken moon form intricate patterns. It has long been supposed that reading these signs can portray the future.
- **Mric Nettor** –*(Mric Net-tor)* Leader of the earthdweller underground communities that were destroyed.
- **Mullgrub** – A multiple legged carrion-feeding grub. A vermin that feeds on dead matter, and can grow to considerable size when uninhibited by predators or sources of dead matter.
- **Multox** – A beast of burden, slow and deliberate, able to carry significant loads, or draw wagons many times its own weight.
- **Narkle** – a dead goblin, who questioned the Badger's authority.
- **Ovalstar** – An Elven City in the time of Ganadon that was too remote to send reinforcements to save Ganadon.
- **Pale Leaf** – a town near Darkleaf Forest in the vicinity of Long Creek and Heartleaf.
- **Palestone** – a form of white or gray obsidian used to make tips for sharp weapons.
- **Papa Theron** – A woodsman and friend to the fae-creatures.
- **Pixie** – A fae-creature, delicate, winged creature of light and cheer.
- **Poraque** –*(Po-Ra-kay)* A leader in one of the underground cities besieged by the goblins of Ric Noar who was enslaved as a result.
- **Raskar Crittooth** – A goblin prince, apparently in league with the Beast King.

- **Ravna** – *(Rav-na)* Known as the Mistress of the Inn, Ravna sees to the well-being of the weary travelers who frequent the Silver Dagger Inn. Unless she is in one of her moods, she tends to take the edge off of Gort's manner, and the patrons of the Inn tend to prefer to deal with her, than risk the dangers of upsetting the volatile Ogre. Ravna is not the first to bear the title of Mistress of the Inn.
- **Red Teeth** – A goblin tribe.
- **Ric Noar** – A goblin prince involved in the fall of thes underground cities: Earthdweller city, Tin Par, and the Red Rock Troll city, Felindah. He made a bargain with one Red Rock Troll as a trick to gain access to the underground cities.
- **Right-of-Blood** – A goblin weregild law that gives goblins the rights to slay one another.
- **Ring of the Judges** – A governing body of Judges, rulers of the Red Rock Troll underground cities. The ring of the judges bear all rights to hear and hold courts and cast judgments, appoint new judges and enforcer the sacred laws written upon the Scroll of Ordinances. At one point the Collector conspired to obtain control of this body and the Scroll of Ordinances, and caused the destruction of Felindah. Each city within the complex of underground cities of a given size and population associated with Felindah, had delegates appointed to the Ring of the Judges, so that each city was represented to some degree within the govering body.
- **Rosewine Pear** – A dark red juicy fruit.
- **Rumleaf** *(Yellow)* – An herb. Often dried and used in medicinal teas.
- **Sagging Bellies** – The Badger's idea of a good name for a goblin tribe.
- **Scribeworms** – Wood-boring worms. They eat intricate patterns into moist dead wood.
- **Scroll of Ordinances** – A scroll bearing the legal rights to rule, ancient laws, and other traditional ordinances held in common among the fallen Red Rock Troll's city-state of Felindah.
- **Seven Hunters** – A cluster of stars that are thought by some to foretell omens when the broken moon and its fragments pass near.
- **Sibyl Bird** – A common forest bird with a white beak and patch of red at its throat, with a prominent and resounding

call, thought by some to foretell one's destiny.

- **Silver Dagger Inn** – A large inn and tavern, deep in the heart of Darkleaf forest. It is located on the edge of ancient trade routes that are seldom used.
- **Siv** – The Barkeep of the Silver Dagger Inn, a forestwalker, with a mysterious past.
- **Skyloc** – *(sky-lock)* A long-necked skittish forest lizard, probably too curious for its own good.
- **Sloth** *(Forest Sloth)* – A shaggy, slow-moving forest animal, that tastes like chicken.
- **Sons of Fire** – A goblin tribe.
- **Soursalt** – A salty sour powdery substance used in curing meats and masking flavors.
- **Southern Human Kingdom** – A common name for the realm of White Bird. Many months journey to the south, from the Silver Dagger and of little consequence to the lands of the north. The kingdom is ruled by a noble caste known as the Velumni. The lower caste of people is known collectively as Rogues.
- **Star-lore** – The practice of looking to the skies as a way to tell stories, legends, and predict the future.
- **Stone Staffs** – A goblin tribe.
- **Strawgrass** – A tender grass that can be used in place of straw. It is easily cut or bruised and unlike other more hearty grasses. A being passing through a field of strawgrass leaves broken stems and a clearly discernable path that is easy to follow.
- **Sweetleaf** – An herb used for smoking, used for calming nerves and relaxing.
- **Talithar** –*(Tal-i-thar)* A dragon of legend and a serpentine constellation of stars.
- **Tannis Per** – A son of Crimson Per.
- **Tia-Pho-Phia** –*(Tia-Fo-fia)* A pixie. Often called Tia for short.
- **Tin Par** – Was the capital city of a complex underground community of earthdwellers who served the red rock trolls beneath Darkleaf.
- **Velumni** – *(Ve-lum-ni)* The human caste of aristocrats, the privileged noblemen of the Realm of White Bird. They are organized according to family, Velumni being the ruling family, from which all other nobles derive their authority. Velumni

can be generous, but most are intent upon keeping and holding power, and gaining more power through a complex series of games and rules they have devised in their kingdom. As a result, often much mischief and conspiracy ensues in the Southern Human Kingdom of White Bird.

- **Vhagua-root** –*(bog-wa root)* A foul-smelling addictive drug, a popular vice among Goblins.

- **Waxbulb Root** – A root that when broken exudes a black colored juice, often used for dyes.

- **Weave (the)** – A power in the earth that beings known as "Weavers" can manipulate as by magic. The Weave is a highly intoxicating powerful force that ultimately destroys those that use its power. It is in and about the world; accessible to beings taught to access it. Most sensible people of the land liken the weave to evil, and weaving as a reckless self-destructive act. The weave affects all races differently and is a subject of great secrecy. All known societies have rules and traditions in place to "deal with" weavers, the most common of which is to hunt down any of its proponents and slay them. Even so, there are some remote (and often hidden) enclaves that still attempt to practice controlling the weave, most often for personal gain and power, which is contradictory to the nature of the Weave and will bring about madness in the Weaver all the more readily. Depending upon the power, natural abilities, training and craftiness of the Weaver, the weave can change and manipulate the powers of nature. It can alter perceptions of the mind. It can enhance perception and heal or it can be used to rend flesh and slay others. Should the weave be used to slay another living being, madness ensues a hundredfold quicker. The Weave can bestow items with power, but at a great cost to the one performing the weave. Likewise talented weavers once could leave the effects of the weave upon the earth itself, this is called (by those who know) "a Tangle".

- **Weaved Gem** – A gemstone given mysterious properties by the Weave.

- **Weaver** – A being (most typically human, elf or red rock troll) capable of tapping into the Weave. Based upon their skill and sanity, they can perform seeming "miracles," though most feats are illusory in nature, manipulating light and mind.

- **White Bird Cove** – The capital city of the realm of White Bird, known commonly as the Southern Kingdom. The High

King of White Bird rules from a grand palace within this city, and is thus the subject of considerable attention from subjects and conspiring Velumni noblemen. White Bird should not be confused with the White Stone Hall, which is in a completely different region of the world, far, far, far to the north of the Southern Human Kingdom.

- **Weregild** – An old goblin name for a primal goblin tribe, unified in a code of savage laws and traditions.
- **White Stone Hall** – A city to the far north, on the edge of avast lake. It is a city of philosophy and sophistication, with aspirations to create a lasting peace between all the different races of the world. All the realms of all accessible lands host consulates and delegations of diplomats in this city. The city was once considered the fore most city of the known world, though of late, the realms to the far south (White Bird, in particular) have begun to question its relevance, due to the legitimate concern that the city is rather inaccessible and was slow to render assistance against the pirates that plagued the Grand River trade route between the White Hall into the Southern Kingdoms.
- **Windy Mountains (the)** – A mountain range that hems in Darkleaf forest to the west and northwest. A home for goblins and stone trolls.
- **Wolvm** –*(wol-vum)* A large and ferocious dog-like predator of the more wild parts of Darkleaf, rumored for its savageness and cunning.
- **Wolvm Claws** – A goblin tribe.
- **World of the Brokenmoon** – The world in which this story takes place. The moon over this world is fractured into many pieces that at times string out across the sky and at other times contract. It is commonly held in the memory of all intelligent beings that the moon was not always so fractured in the time before the great Darkness, but how the races know this or any other notions of the past are forgotten in the mists of time.
- **Worm-Eye** – A Goblin in the raider camp.
- **Yellow Eyes** – A goblin tribe.
- **Yellow-must** – A toxic yellow mold.

the Weave

There is a power bound to world of the Brokenmoon and to the beings that live there. This power is thought to predate the ancient blackness, before recorded history, from the worlds that were. Now, in the world that is, it has unwieldy and deadly consequences for those who dare delve too deeply into its intoxicating undertow. The history of the world of the Brokenmoon has been forever altered by the discovery of this power.

The weave affects all the races and individuals of each race in its own way. For some of the races (and families within given races) it exhibits itself as an extraordinary talent that defies understanding. For others, one must actively pursue its study and hone one's mind to manipulate the weave's powers. This manipulation is known as "weaving." Weaving requires rigorous mental training that takes a great deal of study and patience, under the tutelage of those who guard its secrets with the utmost sobriety.

The power of the weave is intoxicating to the intelligent mind. It is euphoric and addicting, and all other senses become, by comparison, vulgar and painfully dull. A weaver may simply forget to eat, starving himself to death. Whatever the discipline and methods they learned to master the weave, slowly or quickly, depending on the mind, the weaver's mind erodes, until the very act of caring for even the flesh of their own bodies becomes tedious and easy to neglect. They confuse reality with illusions that the weave can conjure and become slaves to the weaver's power. They soon desire nothing but the complete submission to the power that they wield. They want to merge with something they cannot. They bask in its titillating glow until they are withered, having spent their strength on the pursuit of an illusory pleasure. They may become fixated on an object, place, or person that may or may not exist. They may hear things others do not. They may see things that were, but are no longer. They may converse with inanimate objects. They may see things that could be, or they may simply babble incoherently, thinking they are the most eloquent and intellectually powerful beings in the universe. They let their minds float away with the weave's maddening pull, and what remains is always very dangerous. Without conscious understanding of the consequences or while listening to the coaxing of intangible beings only the weaver's can perceive, they could possibly fold matter in upon itself, snuff out life, or devastate an entire city.

It is this reason that the weave is so feared and hated. It is this reason why the weave is no longer taught, save in secret places or under strict controls and always with the constant threat of death at any sign of insanity. None of the common mortal races have ever weaved without either a quick death or eventual decay of the weaver's mind. Once the first weave is started, it's only a matter of time. Some take their own lives before they completely lose control. Other weavers leave their fate up to others who wait in secret to use them for their own purposes or kill them.

Such has inspired the expression, "To weave is death."

Other properties of the weave:
The weave as a weapon

It has been noted by the Red Rock Trolls that when the weave is used as a weapon to destroy life, or harm others against their will (even on non-weaver victims), that the mind of the weaver accelerates greatly towards insanity. When two weavers clash in combat, seldom do either of them leave with their sanity intact. It has been speculated that the minds of all intelligent creatures are somehow connected to the weave, and thus there is some sort of defense or backlash created in the act of snuffing out the life of another. This well-known fact leads most weavers to think of ways to impede or misdirect an enemy rather than obliterate them—of course, when the insanity of the weave inevitably sets in, this is one of the first rules they forget.

The Weaver's Knot

A weaver is strongest in the place where he first weaves. The weave is very sensitive to the weaver's position. In the past, when weavers were formally trained, they were forced to open themselves to the weave in remote places and then sent far from that point of origin, thus severely limiting the weaver's ability to do damage to others with the weave. Thinking that they would be more controllable, the long distance only increased the weaver's craving to weave, thus hastening the impending madness.

Among weavers, the geographic locale where the first weave occurs is called a "weaver's knot;" this is their place of greatest power. A prospective student of the weave, who has yet to perform his first weave is sometimes referred to as "unknotted." An unknotted weaver is not a weaver, and has never performed a weaving, but has studied weaving and in general, the connotation of the term is that they intend to create a weaver's knot when the time is right (which varies according to teacher, mental discipline and choice).

The most advanced unknotted students can detect the weave, feel the weave's effects upon another or an object, and get a general sense of the source of the weave. It is to them like a voice. Just as in a crowd of people a person may hear one loud voice but may not be able to dicern who spoke, unknotted studends can tell from what direction came the weave. Many of the Black Eagles (mentioned later) are unknotted weavers who, understanding the full consequences of the weave, have vowed to have nothing to do with it.

Tangles

The most powerful weavers have had an ability known as "tangling" in which they create a lasting weaving effect over an area, even after the weaver is long gone or dead. Common tangles are misdirection, curses, wards, traps, and illusions. Lesser powerful weavers can invoke these effects only as long as they keep their minds upon the effect, but a true tangle is permanent, unless removed ("ordered" or "untangled"). Tangles are associated with a place and depending on their strength cover a varying area of effect. A whole mountain can be tangled, a cave, a passageway, a forest, a triangular section of the sea, or the plot of a house. Often tangled objects are mistakenly said by common folk to be "jinxed" or "haunted."

Weavers that can tangle the weave are almost unheard of. With the exception of Goblins who have a knack for breaking tangles, weavers that can untangle or "order" a tangle are just as rare. Tangle weaves have been used in the past to lure in weaver hunters, subject them to curses, untimely disappearances, and death. Because the effects of the weave can be felt in a tangle, even without the weaver present, they were commonly used to decoy weaver assassins away from the actual weaver.

Unfortunately, those that master tangles tend to go mad shortly thereafter, so it is not a skill sought out regularly. Often simple tangles occur when a weaver is in the throes of weaver madness. A simple tangle might be a rainbow that appears when a fire is lit in an area, a patch of earth that glows when rains falls upon it, the sound of weeping when passing through an otherwise empty house, and bloodstains of the fallen weaver that simply won't clean up regardless of how many gallons of the Mad Mudwin's Miracle Alchemy Stain remover are used.

Weaved Objects

Weaved objects are seemingly permanent effects put upon an object, instead of a place, like tangles. At one time, it was thought that if weavers merely focused their weaving into objects they could avoid the madness. Sadly, as in most things involving the weave, the opposite was true.

Though the nature of the soul is an unknown in the world of the Brokenmoon, it is commonly believed that a weaved object requires the weaver to leave a piece of himself or herself in the object in question. This soul has likewise been known to exert influence on the bearer of the object. Thus even the madness of weaving can be shared with those incapable of weaving through the use of objects closest to the weaver. Separation of the object from the weaver who created it, often results in the death or immediate maddening of the weaver.

Any object can be weaved, but it must be something of particular importance to the weaver, and something the weaver can keep close at hand. Often it is a weapon, an heirloom like a gem, or something of deep familial importance. Weaved objects have given their bearers great powers, without the need to weave, and at one time powerful aristocrats attempted to force weavers to create objects for their use.

Weaved objects are very difficult to create and usually only are formed in moments of extreme torture and duress or in a need so grave that the weaver has no more desire to continue. Ironically by weaving an object, a part of them is trapped forever in the object, essentially becoming immortalized in that object.

Useful (as opposed to cursed or just plain irritating) weaved objects are very rare, and those that are known in the world are coveted by the most powerful and dangerous beings in the realm.

Maps

The following maps along with several other documents were found in the study of an old Red Rock Troll. They seemed to be written in a combination of modified elvish and the artistic symbolism of the Red Rock Trolls. We have been unable to interpret the symbolism of the maps, but we believe that if you search the pages of the history of the Bean, you will find the keys to translate them.

The first map seems to represent the Land of the Broken Moon with White Stone Hall in the center, surrounded by Darkleaf and the other kingdoms of the time.

On the pages following the map of the Broken Moon, are maps of a more mysterious nature. One seems to represent land above the earth around the Silver Dagger Inn, while the other is more like a treasure map that represents a specific path within the many caverns underground.

As we find more documents and maps, they will be released in future volumes so that you can continue your journey in the Land of the Broken Moon.

-the Authors-

217

Aimee Duncan

Aimee Duncan lives in her own quiet little niche in North Carolina, surrounded by family and a beach or two. There's never been a time when she hasn't been writing, drawing or reading something. This book represents her first venture into published writings. By no means will it be her last.

Travis Hanson

Travis Hanson has resided in Southern California most of his life. He spent 2 years in Argentina where he learned the Spanish language and to love the Spanish culture. He has always had a wonderful imagination and has spent the last 10 years improving his artistic skills to convey the brilliant images within his mind. Currently he is a graphic artist as well as illustrator of several books. His children have provided inspiration for much of his current work and his wife is a constant support to him in his endeavors. This is his first book with Aimee and it surely will not be the last. Bean is very much a part of Travis and will grow with him throughout his adventures.